Her Desirable Defender

Men in Uniform: Marines

M.D. Dalrymple

BOOK ONE

Copyright 2023 M.D. Dalrymple /Michelle Deerwester-Dalrymple

ISBN: 9798395169051

Imprint: Independently published

All images licensed by Canva.com

Formatted by Atticus

All rights reserved. In accordance with the U.S. Copyright Act of 1976, the scanning, uploading, distribution, or electronic sharing of any part of this book without the permission of the author constitutes unlawful piracy of the author's intellectual property. If you would like to use the material from this book, other than for review purposes, prior authorization from the author must be obtained. Copies of this text can be made for personal use only. No mass distribution of copies of this text is permitted.

This book is a work of fiction. Names, dates, places, and events are products of the author's imagination or used factiously. Any similarity or resemblance to any person living or dead, place, or event is purely coincidental.

Bonus Police Ebook

DON'T FORGET TO GRAB your bonus ebook police romance ebook starter! Use the information below to receive *On Patrol*, a pulled from real life short story in your inbox, plus more freebies and goodies!

https://view.flodesk.com/pages/5f74c62a924e5bf828c9e0f3

A hero would sacrifice you to save the world; a villain would sacrifice the world to save you.
A Marine would sacrifice himself to do both.

Contents

1. Cole   1
2. Isis   7
3. Cole   13
4. Isis   16
5. Isis   21
6. Cole   24
7. Cole   30
8. Cole   34
9. Cole   39
10. Cole   42
11. Cole   45
12. Cole   51
13. Cole   56
14. Isis   59
15. Isis   63
16. Cole   68

17.	Isis	76
18.	Cole	83
19.	Isis	87
20.	Cole	93
21.	Cole	102
22.	Isis	107
23.	Cole	116
24.	Cole	123
25.	Cole	131
26.	Isis	135
27.	Cole	139
28.	Isis	144
An Excerpt from Undercover		152
Excerpt from Charming		157
Marine Corps Report		162
About the Author		164
Also By M.D. Dalrymple		165

Cole had to no
have more trainir
States near a beacl
Corporal Maxt
"Corporal, wh
Drake inquirin
Cole's finger tigh
finger did the san
Good Marine.
"West gate, Sar
Both Cole and
as their eyes scan
response.
If it had been a
caused the same r
If Sarge was rad
developed near tl
right after sunset,
No *good* reasor
"We have a rep
from south-soutl
tary insurgents. V
"Roger that. W
Cole slid his ga
"Keep your ey
have company."

Hostiles usuall
ferred weapons w

Chapter One
Cole

He wiped at the damp, sandy grit on his face.

"Hot enough for you, Iron Maxton?"

"Fuck you, Cortes. Your pits are wetter than your sister, and I should know."

"Watch it, Iron Max, before I yank that tongue from your mouth."

Cole tilted his sweaty head toward Private Cortes and grinned. Cortes, to his credit, hadn't moved and kept his rifle high on his chest as he studied the western landscape and the sand that extended to the sea just outside the city of Manama, Bahrain. His code name Iron Maxton was one his men had coined for him, a play on words over his hard-edged exterior and because it sounded a bit like some popular superhero character.

This type of conversation was everyday banter for his unit.

"Then what would I use to lick your sister?"

Private Diego Cortes huffed out a steamy breath as his lips curled into a tight grin.

2

"How much longer [...]
asked.

Fortunately, Cole ha[...]
the corporals before t[...]
squad on night duty, [...]
titerrorism Security T[...]
This one had been lig[...]
but they had been swe[...]
and the entire squad v[...]

He lifted his helmet[...]

"Sgt. Drake said wo[...]
mand wants us out by[...]

Private Cortes lifte[...]
cheeks glistened. They[...]
who burned, peeled, [...]
sunblock he used. C[...]
scarf off his neck. No[...]
in this heat, and adjus[...]
cotton from one spot[...]

"*Oohrah*. I can't wa[...]
long are we on leave?"

The sun shifted a b[...]
the horizon. Cole tigh[...]
Better for the glare, bu[...]
ening shadows as well[...]

Embassy guard sup[...]
but not *that* easy. Co[...]
local insurgents, and [...]

Going home could [...]

"You get ten days, [...]
fornia, until our next [...]
as hot as here."

Diego let a low wh[...]
wait. Ten days, then [...]
vacation."

heavy weaponry, and any engagement this close to the Embassy was a problem.

FAST Team 6 Cheetah's problem to be exact. Their entire duty at the moment was to make sure no rioters, insurgents, or hostiles got too close. Marines were the tip of the spear, meant to stop a threat before it became a threat and the Marines and soldiers inside the Embassy gates had to get involved.

"There." Diego thrust out his chin toward the street.

The haze of dust from the southwest was thicker than the general haze of the day.

"Time to call in the calvary," Cole commented and clicked his radio. "Cheetah Squad. We got a small group of hostiles approaching from the south. Cameron, Sheedy, Nowak, you got our six?"

"Roger that. Non-lethal?"

Cole looked over at Diego, who leaned forward and studied the crowd. His hand shifted from his weapon to his vest, and his entire visage hardened.

"Small cluster of hostiles, non-military," he said in a clipped voice.

"Non-lethal," Cole confirmed.

"Roger that. Stand down unless engaged, over."

"Copy that," Cole responded, moving his hand to the case near his hip. "Over and out."

Just as the small, shouting crowd neared, three Marines in full gear and clear shields at the ready ran from the northwest-side of the Embassy wall.

"What do you have, Corporal?" Lance-Corporal Cameron asked.

Cole pointed. "A crowd of hostiles, look like small-time rioters, about thirty meters out. Probably coming by to ask us to leave."

Cameron spat onto the dust road at his feet. "*Oohrah*. They can ask all they want. They just better ask nicely."

Private Sheedy stepped up next to Cole. He spoke a smattering of broken Arabic, and most of those in Bahrain spoke a bit of English. Cole hoped that between the two, they could convince the rioters to stand down, or at least take their riot away from the Embassy.

Because their standing orders were to draw lethal fire on anyone who threatened the Embassy. There had been too many breaches at embassies in the past, and the Marines weren't fucking around.

The crowd of men neared, stabbing their fists in the air.

A familiar move. This wasn't the first crowd to protest U.S. presence in their capital, and Cole doubted it would be the last.

He looked at Sheedy. "You're on."

Sheedy handed his shield to Cole and stepped in front of him. Keeping his right hand on his baton, he lifted his left hand in greeting and shouted in Arabic.

The rest of the squad tensed, and Cole kept one hand on his radio, ready to call 10-30 if the rest of the squad was needed.

His other hand was on his non-lethal.

A buzzing sound came from overhead – a drone. Unnecessary, most likely, but the detachment command used every excuse to use them. Cole and his men presumed it was to justify their cost.

Right now, though, five Marines against this small crowd that appeared to be civilians were more than enough.

"We don't want you here!" the young man shouted to Sheedy. *Oohrah*, English.

"And we don't want to be here." Cole met the man's tone with his own. "But we've been attached to the embassy, and just as you are trying to protect your people, we have to protect ours. We have no intention of doing anything more than standing here in the dust and sun until they send us home. Unless you do anything that might be misconstrued as attacking the Embassy."

Cole let the last words, a veiled threat, linger and hoped the young man knew enough English to understand.

The man rubbed at his dark day's growth of stubble as his angry eyes glared at the Marines and their equipment. Cole didn't blame him for his anger at all. Hell, he'd be pissed to find this much of a foreign military outside any Embassy in the US.

But they weren't in the US. They were in a war zone and had been called in by the Saudis and their allies directly. They were here by invitation, even if the locals didn't like it.

Sad fact of life.

The shouting died down as the young man continued to glare. Then he turned to his small troupe and shouted something in Arabic, and the crowd marched away.

Cole released a hard breath through his nose.

The last thing he wanted was another highly-publicized embassy conflict.

"Stand down," he told his Marines.

They released their grip on their non-lethals, and Sheedy turned to Cole to retrieve his shield.

"Corporal, I can't wait to leave here. This on-edge shit is for the birds," he said before joining Cameron to head back to their northwest post.

Cole was more of a like mind with Sheedy, with his entire detachment, than anyone might guess. He put on a stern face, but he too wanted to leave the desert and sleep for days. Maybe drink some cold water for the first time in almost a year. Cole tightened his already tight lips.

"*Oohrah* that," Cole agreed with Sheedy as he watched his Marines in their desert BDUs disappear into the dust.

Chapter Two
Isis

Isis really didn't care to go out bar hopping. Her friends, Carly and Deidre, were up for a night of drinks and guys, but that meant seedy bars and bad boys. And Isis was way, way too tired of that scene. Too many lousy boy boyfriends in a row, and after a bad breakup with yet another bad boy, she was done.

Just done.

She was going to be looking for something substantial with anyone else, but she wasn't ready to start looking for that *now*.

But Carly hadn't let up with her texts, and if she didn't go, who knew which bad boy she might take home and let break her heart.

Again.

Carly should be done playing this game, too. Every other weekend on her nights off, though, she wanted to try again.

This time, at least, it was somewhere different. Isis parked her eco-friendly compact and entered through the main door. The bar near the base was called *Easy Company*, a Marine-themed dive with photos and insignia adorning the walls.

Typical.

The bar wasn't too crowded – Isis expected it to be a bit busier for a Friday night – but enough people to keep Carly and Deidre there. They were already seated at a table.

A few of the people, young guys, were probably from the base if their close-cropped hair and stiff postures were any indication.

A couple of older men nursed amber liquid at the end of the bar, and another group of guys, rougher around the edges compared to the neat military nature of the young guys, loitered near the wall. A few other women sat at the bar, as well as other couples and trios out for Friday night drinks to drown their work week sorrows.

They all glanced up at her entrance, and while most of the patrons turned back to their drinks, Isis didn't miss some lingering gazes.

Mainly from the rougher crowd, but also the intense, light blue gaze of one of the clean-cut men. His hair grew a bit longer on top in tight, soft brown curls, and he was tall, taller than the other guys near him.

Those eyes...

If she was looking for a date, that tall, handsome drink of water would have topped her list.

But she wasn't. Let him look. She'd even preen for him, as long as he stayed on his side of the bar.

And if, over the course of the night, her gaze drifted to his tightly packed muscles carved out by military service, then it did.

She might not be looking for a man, but she wasn't one to turn down a decent view.

And this man was the poster boy for the Marine base, she was sure of it.

Her friends had claimed a table between the door and the bar, and Carly took their drink orders.

Isis had asked for a diet soda, but Carly frowned at her, an almost comical look on her rosebud lips.

"Diet soda and rum? Got it."

Isis opened her mouth to protest, but Carly spun around and was heading to the bar before she got a word out. Next to her, Deidre giggled.

"Let it go, Isis. You need to relax and loosen up. You've been too uptight lately." Deidre's face brightened. "You need to get laid!"

Isis slapped the table with her palm, but Deidre cut her off.

"No, really. There's a selection of guys here. If you want uptight like yourself, shoot for one of those guys." Deidre flicked her neon pink-tipped finger toward the military guys. They had to be Marines, Isis guessed, because the local base was a huge Marine base, Camp Pendleton.

Deidre rotated her hand and pointed toward the rougher group. Post-college at best, maybe a bit older, and trying to reclaim their glory days with longer hair, goatees, and rock concert t-shirts.

They reminded her too much of her past loser boyfriends, so they didn't interest Isis at all.

Plus, she was enjoying the view of the tall Marine by the bar.

"Nope, just girl's night tonight."

Carly showed up with drinks in tow. They cheered each other and sipped, and Carly began prying Deidre for information about a recent date she'd had.

Someone put music on the jukebox, and strains of a recent rock song poured through the narrow bar. Isis glanced at the rockers – probably one of their picks. She also noticed how the military group tilted their heads when the music kicked on.

Must be a trained response, Isis mused.

She and her friends became engrossed in Deidre's love life and hadn't noticed several rocker men approach their table.

"Hello, ladies. You looking for company?"

Isis gave the men a tight smile. It was nice that they asked, but as experience had shown her, that usually didn't mean they wanted an answer. Better to play nice and let them down with a kind word.

"Thank you for the offer," Isis said to the man who spoke. His dark brown hair was straight and matched his goatee. "But we're having a girls' night, thanks."

The man's eyebrows lowered briefly to glance at her breasts that tugged her t-shirt tight. So much for being nice. He didn't like her answer.

"Come on. Pretty girls like you? Naw, you shouldn't be alone. Come on and join us."

The man put his hand on Carly's arm, and her wide, frantic eyes shifted from Isis to Deidre and back.

"No thanks," Diedre answered as she tried to lean in front of Carly to block her, but she was at the wrong angle.

"Yeah, we said it's girls' night," Isis said again, hoping to get the guy to release Carly's wrist.

He did, then his pudgy fingers wrapped around her upper arm and brushed against her side-boob.

What the hell? He's touching me? The audacity!

"And I said it looks like you want company." The man's voice held a sharp edge, and Isis's stomach dropped to her feet.

Why were men like this? He was probably drunk off his ass and trying to impress his friends . . .

She shifted, twisting her arm, and tried to break his grip, but it tightened.

Then someone else was standing behind her, and she froze in fear.

"She said no."

The voice was strong and commanding and didn't seem to be coming from another of the rockers.

No, it was the military guys. She could see their group from the corner of her eye, forming a half circle around her and her friends.

Ironically, Isis had never been so grateful to be surrounded by strange men in her life.

The man holding her arm glared at the Marine who spoke. Isis couldn't see who it was, but from the feel of the guy and his voice, he seemed tall. The curly-haired guy, then?

"This doesn't concern you, jarhead. This ain't base, and you don't have any say here."

The Marine shifted, coming nearly next to her.

"I don't, but she does. She said no. And even a man like yourself should understand so basic a word."

"Fuck you."

The Marine moved so quickly that Isis wouldn't have believed it if she hadn't been standing right there. He struck the man's wrist so it broke contact with her, then spun him around and slammed his face down onto their table. The other military guys shoved the rocker's friends away as the curly-haired Marine grabbed the back of the guy's collar, lifted him from the table, and shoved him to his friends.

"Now, either drink nicely or get out if you can't respect the people in here." The Marine's eyes, such lovely blue earlier, were like ice chips as he stared the man down.

"Fuck this. This bar is shit anyway!" he shouted as he led his group of friends from the bar.

One of them spat on the floor at the doorway as they left, and the entire bar breathed a collective sigh of relief.

The young Marine turned to Isis. Even though his eyes had softened slightly as he looked at her, the hard lines of his face and the sharp edge of his jaw remained.

He bobbed his head slightly. "Sorry for the intrusion, miss," he said politely.

His friends dipped their chins and mumbled their apologies as well.

Isis didn't miss how Carly and Deidre grinned at each other.
Oh no.

"Thank you for that," Isis told him, unable to tear her gaze away from those piercing blue eyes.

"Miss," he said again with another quick bob of his head and turned away.

Only then did Isis start breathing again.

Chapter Three
Cole

Cole stepped away from the situation at the table and returned to the bar with his fellow Marines. His body might have turned away, but his mind was stuck on that gorgeous strawberry-blonde woman who handled herself so well when that fucker put his hands on her.

It had taken Cole everything in his power not to strangle the guy where he stood.

Cole had noticed the woman when she entered and joined her friends. Tanned and on the slightly slender side, with beach waves and sun-kissed cheeks, she had a look about her that she didn't quite belong in a dive bar off a Marine base.

So he hadn't taken his eye off her.

He had elbowed Lance-Corporal David Sorell and Private Nowak when the roughneck, who was too big for his britches, approached the table. When the lug touched the first woman, Cole and his squad headed over. Only five of his squad were in the bar, and thankfully not Sgt. Drake, who would have ripped Cole a new one for instigating violence. Drake himself might have a military offense record as long as Cole's arm, but the man ran a tight ship with his Marines.

Fortunately, the lug had taken the hint after having his head slammed into the table, and he and his cronies left.

Then he had to speak to the woman. Had he been left nearly speechless by the presence of a woman before?

Nope. Not Iron Maxton.

Not until today.

Not until she turned that inquisitive green (*or was it gray?* In the dim light, he couldn't tell) gaze on him, and he forgot how to speak.

Nowak had poked him in the back and Cole managed to bark out an apology, which was all he had. The woman smiled and accepted his apology for the rude interruption, and then he left.

Otherwise, he would have continued to gape at her.

Hard Iron Maxton bowled over by a woman in a dive bar.

He could hear Nowak and Sorell snickering behind him.

He'd never hear the end of it.

"What happened to your voice, Corporal? Lose it on the way to the table?"

"Shut your face, Sorell."

More snickering.

"Why didn't you give her your name? Missed opportunity!" Sorell laughed.

"You're gonna miss out on that sweet kitty? Go for it, Corporal!" Nowak added.

Sorell slapped Cole's upper back as he cackled.

Making sure to keep his eyes averted from the three women at the center table, Cole lifted his beer bottle to his lips and finished it.

More jokes from his squad.

Yeah, he'd have to go. He wasn't in the mood.

It might be their last real night out before they deployed again, but he was done. Other than a random hook-up, why try to approach the sun-kissed woman when he was leaving in two days? It wasn't fair to her, and he wasn't in the place to offer anything more to a woman.

Not even to this angel in a dive bar.

Gripping the bar edge, Cole huffed out his breath and pushed off the bar counter.

"Okay, Marines. You're on your own. You okay to get back to base? Uber or something if you need a ride. Don't drive drunk. Don't need any Cheetahs getting a DUI right before we roll out."

Nowak gave him a mock salute. "*Oohrah,* Corporal."

With a tight smile, Cole turned and headed for the door.

He allowed himself one quick, final glance at the woman who was chatting with her friends, then ducked out the sagging, sea-water-stained doorway.

But he didn't rush toward the base across the street. Instead, he perched on the short stone wall to collect his thoughts and breath in the fresh, cool sea air. He'd miss it when he went back to the desert.

The blonde had intrigued him. Too bad he was deploying.

Chapter Four

Isis

Isis couldn't keep her mind on her friends gushing over the Marines who had come to their aid. After dissecting the scenario with pristine and intense analysis, Carly and Deidre debated if they should offer to have the military guys join them. After Deidre's debacle of a recent date, she was as eager as Carly, but Isis was not.

"Come on, Is. I know you've had a slew of bad guys, but these are good guys!"

Carly pointed toward the group of Marines, and Isis couldn't help but notice that the taller curly-haired man, the one who had dealt with the annoying rocker guy, was no longer there. Bathroom?

Either that or he had left.

Isis sighed.

Not that she wanted to try to meet a new guy. She was burnt out.

"You know what they say about military guys. They can be the worst," Isis tried to argue, but after what had transpired moments ago, she didn't believe her own rhetoric.

"Come on," Carly urged.

Isis glanced at her drink. It was nearly gone, and the encounter with the hairy man had chased away any buzz she might have been trying to start.

Isis sighed again.

"I'm gonna go. You guys want to hang out with the Marine hotties, and I'm going to be a downer. Plus, I have to get stuff done before the library opens tomorrow."

"Hey! I thought you said you weren't working tomorrow!" Diedre protested.

Isis shrugged and pushed her glass to the center of the table.

"I'm not, officially, but I have to drop some stuff off and get a room ready for Monday. I don't want to scramble to finish it on Monday morning."

Carly blew out a breath that made her light brown bangs bounce in the air. "Fine. Party pooper. I'll call you tomorrow and tell you about the fun we had with our men in uniform."

Isis raised an eyebrow and danced her gaze to the clean-cut men laughing near the bar.

Yeah, better to let everyone have their fun. She was a party pooper. Isis leaned in and hugged Carly, then Diedre.

"Be safe, text me when you get home, and be sure to give me all the details."

They promised, and Isis dropped two fivers on the table as she left.

She might have stayed if Blue Eyes were still there, but he never returned.

Probably better for her anyway. She didn't need any complications right now.

Isis stepped out into the cool night air.

And nearly tripped over the blue-eyed Marine.

Cole

Cole had risen and was standing near the stone wall, taking in a final view of the moon reflecting on the ocean, when someone crashed into him from behind.

Out of reflex, he reached out his arms to catch the person before they fell, and he froze when he found the tanned blonde woman in his arms.

What the hell?

"Oh, I am so sorry!" she said as he caught her, then her green eyes rose to his face. "Oh my God! It's you!"

Cole couldn't stop the smile that slid across his lips. "And it's you," he teased back. But he didn't let her go. His arms were frozen.

She stared back at him for a moment before pressing her slender hand on his chest.

"Umm, I'm okay. I'm not going to fall or anything."

Cole started and moved his arms. "Oh, right. Sorry."

She shook her head slightly, and her smile, a bright toothy smile that threatened the sun's heat split her wide lips. He noticed that her lower lip was fuller than her upper lip and had a sudden desire to know what her lips tasted like.

Get control, Marine!

Straightening, Cole stepped back a half-step.

The woman flipped her hair over her shoulder. "Thank you again for getting rid of that guy. He was . . ."

"A brash, rude lug. No problem. He should never have interrupted your night out."

The woman's smile slipped a bit, and she shrugged. "Well, that might be the pot calling the kettle black because my friends are planning on asking to join your friends for drinks."

This time, Cole's smile was wide on his face. So much for Hard Maxton.

"I have the feeling they won't mind. They are getting ready for deployment, and most guys want something to, uh . . . ."

How could he put this nicely in a way appropriate for a civilian? His mind was not functioning.

"As a send-off?" she finished for him with her lips curling to into her cheek. Her eyes sparkled in the lights of the flickering bar sign.

God, she's beautiful . . .

"Yeah. Let's put it that way."

"Why aren't you in with your friends? Did the hairy guy ruin it for you?"

He raised an eyebrow and looked down at her. "I could ask the same of you. Leaving a bit early for girls' night."

She shrugged again and cut her eyes to the side. Something was going on with her, more than an interruption by some rude bar patron.

"I wasn't really in the mood to bar hop. Not really looking for a guy or a relationship right now."

Cole glanced back at the bar. "Not really the place one goes to looking for a relationship."

"I didn't say we were smart or looking for a good relationship," she joked, and Cole laughed lightly.

Beautiful and clever.

Shit. He was smitten. One meeting, one conversation, and he knew he would take this with him on deployment.

"What about you? If you aren't looking for *entertainment* before deployment, why hit the bar?"

He shrugged like she had, and even though it might come across as wrong, he decided to be honest. Iron Maxton wasn't known for his tact, after all. The term hard wasn't just for his jawline.

"If I got lucky, then I got lucky. But I'm not looking for a relationship either. Not with an eight-month deployment coming up."

She glanced around the parking lot where a few cars squatted in the dim moonlight. Then she looked back at him.

"What do you do, like your job in the Marines?"

He couldn't help but puff up his chest a bit. If nothing else, he was proud of what he did as a Marine.

"I'm part of FAST – Fleet Anti-terrorism Security Team. We do support for all parts of the military as security escorts. We get in and out fast, get it?" His smile twitched when she nodded. "My squad, Cheetah, is on embassy security reinforcement."

"So you, like, guard embassies?"

Cole pursed his lips at her basic assessment of his duty. "Yeah. Pretty much."

She looked around the parking lot again. Was she looking for someone? Then those intense gray-green eyes landed on him. His breath caught.

"I'm Isis Jennings," she said and extended her hand.

He took it politely and shook it, and an electric surge shot up his arm at her touch. "Cole. Corporal Cole Maxton."

Chapter Five
Isis

STANDING NEXT TO COLE in the dim parking lot lights, he appeared even taller than Isis had previously thought. He was well-muscled, more lean-muscled due to his height, and his defined chest muscles bunched under his dark blue polo shirt when he moved. The ferocious line of his jaw was disrupted only by a gentle cleft in his chin, and Isis had to suppress the urge to brush her fingertip against it.

Damn, he's cute.

Isis shot her gaze toward the parking lot where her small car sat two spaces over. He had said he wasn't looking for anything serious, and that he was deploying soon. And while she had downplayed Deidre's comment about needing to get laid, her friend wasn't exactly wrong.

If he wasn't looking for a relationship, maybe this was exactly what she needed to get over the hump of her previous relationship and have some fun. She deserved it, didn't she?

The only question was if Cole was up for a fling.

From the way his eyes roved over her face and tight-fitting t-shirt, she believed he was.

But taking him to her place was out of the question, and if he was a Marine, he couldn't take her back to his.

They stood quietly outside in the clear salty night air, gazing at each other until Isis realized she was forgetting to breathe.

She had passed a small motel on the way here – most likely for the family of stationed Marines.

It seemed so cliche – getting a motel room for a one-night stand, but damn, he was hot. She had felt the magnetic pull of him from the moment she entered the bar, and this was a guaranteed no no-strings attached. Just what she needed right now.

The question for her was – was she bold enough to ask?

Hell yeah, why not?

She inhaled the refreshing tang of salty air.

"Do you want to go somewhere?" she asked.

His bright blue gaze narrowed slightly. "Somewhere?"

Ugh, he was going to make her say it.

"I'm not looking for anything. Neither are you, but I'd like company, and you can get a send-off before your deployment. I saw a motel down the street . . ."

Her words drifted off, and she let the question linger between them. His face shifted a bit, some of the tension lessening, and it was like all that sweet, salty air was sucked away. Her heart fluttered, freakin' *fluttered*, in her chest.

"Are you sure? This isn't like a reward or something for in there?" His face twisted up slightly as he jerked his thumb to the bar.

She shook her head. "Not a thank you. Just a, well, fling. One night. No strings. You leave the country, and I return to my job and everyday life."

Cole's face softened again.

"Where do you work?" he asked.

Isis wasn't expecting that question. "The library. I'm a library assistant."

The expression on his face shifted, but she didn't understand his expression or why he asked the question. Did it matter what her job was?

No, it didn't. Maybe he was trying to express an interest in her life or calm her nerves with small talk. Or avoid an entanglement if she were somehow associated with the Marine base? None of those were an issue.

"How can I say no to an offer like that from someone as stunning as you?"

The heat of her blush burned up her chest, and she was glad for the dim light so he couldn't see the effect his words had on her.

Isis cleared her throat. "My car's right over here." She pointed.

Without looking away, he slid his hand down her arm and clasped her fingers. It was as if he had touched her core with the heat that surged down her to her knees.

"Lead the way," he said in his rolling tone that sent an electric thrill to her heart.

Chapter Six

Cole

They made more small talk as she drove the block to the motel. Cole asked more about her work, and Isis answered with detail. It was obvious she loved her work, and her excitement resonated with him.

His work as security for the Marines was always tinged with a measure of violent desperation and darkness, a necessary evil in an unstable world. He might be protecting the US and the innocent, but he did so with an M16.

To hear Isis talk about her work, changing the world with books instead of bullets, with reading programs instead of military missions, was like listening to a fantasy tale.

As she spoke, Cole felt a sense of pride, not only in her work and the importance of it, but that because of his work, she was able to do hers.

She turned into the parking lot of the motel. Thankfully, several other cars littered the lot outside the two-story building, and she parked near the blinking sign that read Office.

As she leaned to open her door, he rested his palm on her hand. The heat between them was undeniable and his heart skipped a beat in a moment of panic.

Can I stop with one night? Can I accept no-strings attached?

He'd deal with that goat rope when it happened.

"What are you doing?" he said, stopping her. "I'll get the room."

"But it was my idea."

"Consider it an honor thing. I couldn't live with myself if I let the woman I was with pay for a room."

She tilted her head as if to say okay, and he exited the car, stretching his long limbs out of the compact car, and strode to the office. He returned with a keycard – surprisingly high-tech for a no-tell motel. Second floor, near the end. If they opened the window, they would hear the ocean's crashing waves across the street. Not the worst place he had ever slept, not by a long shot.

Cole glanced over at Isis as she parked.

Not that they'd do much sleeping. Not if he had anything to say about it. His cock throbbed under his zipper at the thought of her in bed with him, of her long, tanned legs, of her calling out his name.

Fuck.

His cock was rock hard against his jeans.

They had to get in that room. The suddenness of it all struck him like lightning, and he needed her. Now.

His dick pulsed again, and as he got out of the car and rushed to open her door, he didn't care if she saw his hard-on under his pants.

He just had to have her.

Without waiting for her to stand upright out of the car, he whipped her into his arms and kissed her, pressing her against her vehicle, trapping her with his body as his lips slanted over hers.

She tasted like sweetness, soda, rum, sexiness, heat, and his cock throbbed achingly against her hip. Isis took that as an invitation, and as his tongue ravaged her mouth, her hand slid to his jean-encased dick and curved around his swollen member. He groaned into her mouth.

It had been way too long for him. He'd bust a nut if he didn't get her upstairs.

Dragging his lips away, he shoved the car door closed and led her up the stairs and into their room for the night.

He thrust her into the room and kicked the door shut, then pressed her up against him. Cole lowered his face until his lips were a breath from hers.

"Are you sure about this?" he asked in a ragged voice.

Oh, god, please say yes . . .

Isis nodded. "Oh yes, I'm sure."

That was all he needed. His lips landed on hers again, licking and sucking. They tore at their clothes as they stumbled over each other toward the bed. They separated their lips only long enough for Cole to whip his shirt over his head.

Isis did the same, and her breasts, full enough to slightly overfill her lacy bra, bounced as she moved. Cole groaned and lifted his hand to cup one luscious mound. Then he tugged the cup down and exposed her nipple to move his mouth to her breast.

She cupped the back of his head as his lips and tongue toyed with her nipple. Gasping at his attention, she gripped his head harder, and his cock throbbed painfully.

Cole moved his lips up to her neck, kissing the tender underside of her jaw as he worked his jeans down and off, kicking off his shoes at the same time.

Her lean fingers did the same, sliding her jeans down her hips and over her well-formed thighs.

Then her pants were off and they were naked, skin pressed against skin, the wet tip of his dick searching for her opening.

He moved her toward the bed as his hand squeezed between them. His finger found the cleft between her legs, the dampness of her pussy, and slid his finger to her clit. She moaned into his mouth as he brushed his fingertip over it a few times, and his engorged cock pulsated.

He couldn't wait any longer.

"I need you, Isis. Now."

Isis

Isis loved the desperation and longing in his voice. It was driving her crazy. When was the last time someone had needed her this much, had made her feel this excited, this titillated, from kissing and touching?

Damn, Cole knew how to make her body sing.

That was something she hadn't experienced in so freakin' long.

Her hands played over his chest, over the defined muscled and the light smattering of curly hair that narrowed as it crested down his trim waist.

God, he was in perfect shape. Everything about him was tight.

The sheer force of his need drove her excitement higher, and she reached her hand down to his dick again, this time bare, a mix of hot velvet and steel, and squeezed slightly. He groaned deep in his chest and dropped his chin.

"Fuck, Isis. I need you now. I need –"

"I need you, Cole. I need you inside me."

Cole didn't hesitate. Isis opened her thighs as he drove her backward onto the soft bedspread and thrust his hips. His swollen dick parted her womanly lips, dipping inside her, then diving deeper. He shoved himself to the hilt, filling her completely, and she threw her head back into the bedding with a gasp.

Each stroke was like an electric charge through her, and as he pulled out, the tip of his cock dragged over that one spot in her sheath that brought her to the brink of madness. She curled her fingernails into his bare shoulder as he pulled out, then squeezed in again and again in a steady cadence.

He didn't close his eyes – instead, he studied her face and dropped his gaze to her quivering breasts that jiggled with each thrust. Then his eyes, those shockingly clear blue eyes, found hers again.

The way he looked at her as his body joined with hers over and over was almost tender, and she closed her eyes and let her mind spin out of control.

His dick, his movements, his hands by her side, everything about him made her tingle as if he already knew her body and what to do and how to move to make her body shudder in euphoria. She moaned her pleasure loud enough for him to hear. He narrowed his gaze so his intense blue eyes snapped like they were electric.

"Is that good for you, Isis?" he said breathlessly. "God, you feel good."

His words made every part of her tingle. She slid her fingertips from his shoulder to his sharp jawline and back.

"Yeah, babe. You make me want to scream."

"Then scream for me. Is. Scream as loud as you can."

His words sent her over the edge. His hard, lean-muscled body and throbbing cock brushed her g-spot in one move and clit with another, overloading her senses and radiating from her slit up through the rest of her body. Her mind exploded in a field of colors and electric ecstasy moments before her body followed.

"Cole!" she shouted through gritted teeth. "Oh my God, Cole!"

She clenched her thighs as she came, fierce and dripping, and gripping him tight against her. That was all he needed.

The thrusting of his hips changed, ground harder and quickened, in and out, dragging inside her, through her. His tempo made him pant, a deep-throated, grumbling pant. Under her hands, his shoulder muscles shifted, tightening as he arched his back and orgasmed, his entire body rigid in his moment.

It was the only time he closed his eyes.

He dropped his head so his forehead brushed hers and panted hotly against her cheek. Isis curled her hand against the back of his neck, holding him close.

They might only have this one moment, this one night, but she didn't want it to end.

Chapter Seven

Cole

"I feel like I should thank you or something," Cole said in a low voice as he rolled to Isis's side.

His naked body, long and dangling off the end of the cheap motel bed, pressed against hers. He should get dressed, call an uber and leave, yet the feel of her skin and his heated contentment outweighed better sense. He liked the feel of her and didn't want to leave.

Dangerous territory, he thought.

She giggled lightly as he brushed her hair off her damp brow. "No. Then I'd need to thank you. I needed that."

She stretched languorously, and he roved an appreciative eye over her lean form. Everything was perfectly proportioned. And tanned. Did she sunbathe nude?

Tanning bed, dumbass, he cursed himself. She doesn't go to nude beaches or anything.

His dick, however, liked that idea and flexed.

Isis noticed and brushed her hand over the sticky length.

Then he froze.

Oh my God. No condom. . .

"Umm," he struggled to come up with the words as he lifted himself on his elbow and looked down at her face. That full bottom lip, her green-gray eyes (*they were both!*), distracted him as he tried to ask the awkward question.

Her strawberry blonde eyebrows rose on her forehead.

"Umm, what?"

"We didn't use. . . I mean, I didn't have . . ."

Fuck. He could gun down the enemy and yell at his subordinates, but asking her about birth control?"

Isis evidently wasn't bothered. "I'm on the pill." She moved her hand so her palm pressed against his chest. Her arm pushed her breasts up and gave her fantastic cleavage. "So you don't need to worry."

He shook his head. "Not that. No, I mean that, but also, it was poor form. I should have asked beforehand. I was just so . . ."

Cole didn't finish his sentence. He lowered his head and kissed her full on the lips. Light and tender, so different from their rough kisses before lovemaking.

Isis pulled back slightly. "Excited. You were excited. I was too. It's okay."

He grinned and her lips mirrored his. He couldn't help himself. He kissed her again. Her sweetness, the taste of her was like the coolest, purest water in the dry, hot desert. He'd never get enough.

So dangerous.

Isis

"How late can you stay?" Isis asked. "I can drop you off at the base so you don't have to call an Uber."

Her head rested on Cole's naked chest, and he played with a lock of her hair. He hadn't scrambled to bail on her once he came, and here he was with his arms around her still.

"Are you in a rush? Do you have anywhere to be?" he asked, his voice as lazy as the gentle movements of his fingers.

She grinned into his chest and curled against him. "Nowhere but here with you. I have to head into work for a bit tomorrow late morning. But nothing before then. You? You got a time you got to be back on base?"

He shook his head. She loved how the tight curls atop his head caught in the dim light by the bed and the cleft in his chin. In addition to having a lean body with defined muscles that rivaled Adonis, he was cute.

"Not until 5:30 am. Well, maybe before that, so I can change for Reveille."

"Reveille?"

"Like the Marine's alarm clock. They play the bugle tune over the PA system, and our day begins."

"5:30 am?" Isis asked. "Man, I am not a morning person. I don't have to be at the library until 8:30 most days. I'm impressed."

One feathery eyebrow rose on his forehead. "Really? Everything a Marine does, and getting up at 5:30 in the morning is what impresses you?"

Isis didn't stop the giggle that bubbled inside her.

"Hey, take what you can get."

Cole's arm tightened around her as his cock brushed her leg. "Well, since we don't have anywhere to be for several hours and you offered, I'll take what I can get."

Then he slid down the bed and maneuvered himself between her thighs. She looked down at his earnest face between the vee of her thighs.

"Is this what you want to get?"

His fingertips parted her lower lips, and his tongue flicked over her slit. She moaned.

Cole lifted his head slightly and his teasing gaze peered at her from between her thighs.

"I get this first. Then I'll take all I can and more."

His tongue found her clit, first sliding over in long sweeps, then flicking it, changing it up until Isis gripped the bedspread and moaned.

"Oh, Cole."

A vibrating quiver bloomed lower in her belly and surged down her legs and up through her breasts to make her head spin. Her nipples grew taut as she whipped her head back and forth.

Then Cole wrapped his firm lips around her clit and sucked lightly. Isis screeched her pleasure and arched off the bed. Her mind shot into another dimension as waves of erotic pleasure washed over her.

Then he sucked again and her hands found his head, gripping his curls as he screamed.

"Cole! Oh my *GOD–*"

Her world exploded, and she fell back to the bed and earth. As she tried to collect her mind, hell, remember her own *name*, Cole slid back up her body, his stiff cock searching for her entrance.

He pressed his lips to her cheek as he slid into her swollen, throbbing sheath, and she shuddered as he thrust deep inside her.

"If we only have tonight, Isis, I'm going to take all I can."

Chapter Eight
Cole

He satisfied his cock and her body one more time that night before they dozed in each other's arms.

Cole had remembered to set an alarm – it was about the only damn thing he remembered to do.

Never had he been so spent and so satisfied all at once.

Whatever it was about Isis, she had managed to crack his stern demeanor and make him senseless. Why the fuck had he met her right before he deployed? And why had he agreed to no strings attached? Because despite any other intentions, she had driven rappelling hooks deep in him, and he was falling hard.

His last thought as his eyelids slammed shut was that he could live like this, with Isis in his arms, forever.

When his alarm sounded before the sun kissed the horizon, he groaned and reached over to shut it off. Isis slid from his grasp and moaned in protest of waking.

"What time is it?" she grumbled in her sleepy voice.

Cole leaned into her and kissed the top of her head.

"Consider it Reveille. Time to start the day."

He sat up and she rolled to the other end of the bed and covered her eyes.

"How are you so perky in the morning?" The last word was more of a mumble, and Cole chuckled lightly.

Naked, he jumped out of bed and stepped to the other side as he collected his discarded clothes.

"I'll be right back," he said as he kissed her cheek.

He yanked on his jeans and shoes and grabbed his wallet. He walked bare-chested into the misty early morning air toward the machines he'd seen behind a glass door next to the office.

His keycard worked to open it, another impressive high-tech aspect to this forgettable motel, and he went right to the coffee machine.

Three minutes later, he was back in the room, setting his cup down on the table and handing out one to her.

Bleary-eyed with mussed hair, Isis propped herself up on her elbow and accepted the cup. She pried open one eye to check out the coffee and sniffed.

Cole sat in the worn, padded chair next to the bed.

"I didn't know how you take it, but last night you seemed to be drinking a soda, so I guess a bit of sweetness was a good idea."

She sipped – cream and extra sugar – as Cole reached his long arm across the table and grabbed his.

"You noticed my drink last night?" she asked after swallowing.

Cole grinned and dipped his head. Probably too much information – did that sound stalker-ish?

Then he lifted his eyes and looked at her beautiful morning disheveled form.

Damn. He could stare at her all day.

"Part of the job. To notice things. Hard to shut off when I'm not in uniform."

Isis took another sip, and her green-gray gaze peered at him over the rim of the paper cup. Cole started leaning in toward her, then caught himself, settled back into the chair, and took another sip of coffee. Not bad, and he'd had much worse.

"I'm going to finish getting dressed. Can you still drive me back to base or –" he pointed over his shoulder as if an Uber driver was already in the parking lot.

He felt like an ass asking, but he also wasn't about to presume anything.

Isis sat up, set her cup on the battered bedside table, and reached for her shirt. She tugged it on and her head popped out of the tight neckline, a slight, sleepy smile on her face.

"Yeah. Yeah, I'll drive you back. I just gotta finish waking up."

They finished dressing and Cole crammed his long legs back into her compact for the short drive back to base.

The drive was quieter than it had been the night before. Cole wasn't certain if it was tiredness, awkwardness, or the fact that this was the end of their amazing night that held their tongues.

"Thank you for this," he finally said as she pulled past the security checkpoint for the base. "This was quite the send-off."

She turned the steering wheel when he pointed and pulled into a long parking lot.

"It was fun. I'm glad we took the chance. Now you can go wherever you're going, and hopefully I'll get my life back on track. I think this night worked well."

Cole stiffened. He hadn't quite expected her to say that. He had been more invested in their night than she, evidently. But he put a tight smile on his face and leaned into her.

"Have a great day at the library," he said, then cupped the back of her head and pressed her lips to his.

A final kiss. A full-lipped, tongue diving, memorable kiss.

In a rush, he opened the door and unfolded himself from the seat.

He had to get out of the car before he said or did something stupid.

Isis

Isis gripped the steering wheel, and from the corner of her, eye watched him leave.

Everything inside her screamed to open her mouth, say something or do something, but in the end, she sat in her car and Cole left.

The feel of his kiss lingered warm on her lips, and as the car door slammed shut, she reached up her fingertip to touch that warmth.

Cole was nothing like she expected, nothing like she thought when she asked him to go to the hotel.

A good lover? No, a great and attentive lover. He made sure she came at least once, or twice, before he got his rocks off. This hadn't been a quickie night in a hotel for him – last night had been an experience.

And he could have asked to leave right after that first time and not worry about any walks of shame in the morning. Instead, he had set an alarm and slept entwined with her all night.

Who did that?

Her gaze flicked to Cole's toned backside, fit and lean in his jeans and polo shirt, until he disappeared into the foggy darkness near his building.

And he was gone.

Isis dropped her head to the steering wheel. She had offered a one-night stand, no strings attached, and no matter how much she regretted that offer now, she did not regret the night.

Hell no.

That was a night she would remember for the rest of her life. His riveting blue eyes, his muscled shoulders, his light brown curls on his head and lower . . .

Even that last kiss was memorable. Not a peck on the cheek, but a full, possessive kiss. One that was meant to be memorable.

A bugle call sounded over a loud PA system. *Reveille,* Cole had called it. Time for the Marines to wake up and start their day.

Time for her to leave.

Isis took a deep breath, turned the steering wheel around, and headed back the way she came.

Chapter Nine
Cole

Cole reached the edge of the building deep in the morning haze and paused to look back. He let out a heavy sigh, knowing it was unlikely that he'd see her again. One night, no strings. That was the agreement.

She was gone.

The thought left a bitter taste in his mouth as he made his way past the metal double doors and into the barracks.

Bright lights illuminated the stark industrial tile and walls, which was enough to wake up anyone.

As he strode down the narrow hallway, he couldn't tear his thoughts from her. She was so different from anyone he'd ever met. Her eyes were like gray mists on the mountains, and her smile lit up even their dim motel room.

And while he wanted to see her again, that freaking agreement and his deployment made it nearly impossible.

He paused and leaned against the wall, pressing his fingertips into his closed eyes.

He hadn't even gotten her number!

Fuck.

It was like she had vanished into thin air.

That he regretted immensely, though he regretted nothing else of the night. How had he missed getting her digits?

Fuckin' idiot, he cursed himself.

He knew he wouldn't forget her, no matter how hard he tried. She was unforgettable.

Dax Cameron found him that way in the hall.

"Hey, brother! What happened to you last night? You took off and never came back."

Cole dropped his hands and turned his face toward Cameron's shit-eating grin. He was clad only in khaki briefs as he worked his way back from the bathrooms.

Since Cole didn't answer, Cameron's grin widened.

"Unless you found a ride with that blonde from last night. She left her friends to us, and if both of you disappeared . . . and you're still in the same clothes from last night."

Dax waggled his thick brown eyebrows suggestively.

Cole rolled his eyes. He wasn't the only observant one. As much as it kept them alive in the Middle East, he hated that trait now.

"Come on. You got to change before mess, and then Lieutenant Jackson wants to review the mission before we deploy tomorrow. And you still gotta pack."

Cole groaned and pushed his body off the wall. Dax followed him as they walked back to the barracks.

"What is up with you? I've never seen you in such a state. Where's Iron-Max?"

Cole went to his footlocker and twisted the lock. He tried to focus on the task at hand and grabbed his BDUs for the day, ignoring Dax's questions.

He had to get Isis out of his mind. Hard Maxton was heading back to the desert, and he needed his wits about him.

The desert would tear him to pieces if he was soft. Better to push any memories of Isis to the side.

But the next day was a blur – Cole barely registered his fellow soldiers' goodbyes and the last-minute preparations for the mission. Even Lt. Jackson had looked at him cross-eyed during their briefing. Cole did everything he could to push Isis from his thoughts.

But as soon as he boarded the transport plane, his mind drifted back to her. He wondered what she was doing at that moment, if she was thinking about him, and if he would ever see her again. He couldn't shake the feeling that he had missed out on something great.

Then he was in the Middle East, guarding another embassy under his Special Forces FAST duty. Days turned into weeks, and weeks turned into months. Most days, he kept his mind on his duties, but at night, when he rested on his cot and sweated through his clothes, his thoughts always wandered back to her.

Chapter Ten
Cole

One hazy, hot day, mere weeks before they were to head back to Pendleton and cool ocean breezes, Cole smacked his lips together, trying to get the sandy grit out of his mouth as he organized his gear – ten more days.

And even though he had nothing to go back to, his mind had worked out how he might find Isis. He could try the bar and see if the bartender or somebody knew her. She worked for the library, which had to be near the bar, in the same town or one nearby. He could check out the libraries, their parking lots, and look for the white compact...

"Hey, Iron-Max, I can get her number."

Cole lifted his eyes, surprised by Private Nowak's sudden comment.

Nowak was grinning, obviously bemused by the expression on Cole's face.

"What are you talking about?" Cole asked, raising an eyebrow at the Marine crouched on the cot across the tent.

"The girl from the bar," Nowak clarified and laid back on the hard cot. "The one with the bright hair and nice ass. The one you left with."

Cole had tried too hard to push Isis from his mind and accept that he probably wasn't going to be able to find her, and to hear Nowak might have her number threw him into a spin.

His hard shell cracked easily on the weight of any mention of Isis.

So much for Iron Maxton.

A reference to her was like a cold wave of water washing over his sun-baked skin.

Rumors of his night with Isis had made the rounds with his squad, and he still wasn't hearing the end of it.

Nevertheless, Cole was intrigued. He tried to play nonchalant as he brushed more eternal sand off his cot.

How did sand get everywhere?

"What do you mean you can get her number?"

Nowak cackled. "I knew that would get your interest. You haven't spoken to her at all, have you? Sorell and some of the guys have called home on the SAT phone, but not you. I guessed you didn't get her number. How does that even happen?"

Cole wasn't about to mention the no-strings agreement he had with Isis. He grimaced and gave a pat answer.

"I just didn't think about it, getting ready to deploy and all."

"Mm-hmm." Nowak didn't believe him – that much was obvious – but didn't press the issue. "We hung out with her friends for the rest of the night. Not that you knew that, seeing as you were otherwise occupied –"

A pair of Cole's rolled-up socks struck his face. Cole had excellent aim. "Shut your hole about it."

"Ohh, sensitive. Not the Iron Maxton I know. Anyhow. Sorell and I got their numbers. I'm sure when we get back, I can text one of them and get her number when we get back stateside."

Cole hated how his heart soared at that news, and he swallowed it back down. He'd never show any emotion. Not to his Marines, not about Isis. He cleared his throat.

"Yeah, well, I'll think about it."

Nowak looked over at Sorell, who had just stepped into the tent, sand drifting off him like hot snow.

"He'll think about it," Nowak said to Sorell.

David sat down hard on his cot, unbuckled his vest, and unbuttoned his BDU shirt. His khaki t-shirt was soaked through with sweat.

"Think about what?" he asked.

"The girl. The one he was with before we deployed."

David looked up at Cole, and his wide mouth smiled so far it seemed to swallow his entire face.

"Oh ho ho. Naw, he wants it. He's just playing tough. Iron Maxton, as always. He wants it. Look at him."

Cole's cheeks burned hot with embarrassment. He hadn't realized that he had been obvious about his attraction to the girl. He glanced away, trying to hide his discomfort.

"I don't need her number," Cole protested, trying to sound disinterested as he moved around some clothing in his trunk. "She's probably taken anyway. It's been eight months. It's not like she's waiting for me. It wasn't like that."

Nowak snorted, obviously not believing him. "Whatever you say, brother. But I'll text you the number, just in case. I got the hookup."

Cole slammed the trunk closed and threw himself onto his cot. He closed his eyes and tried to ignore Sorell and Private Nowak snickering in the background.

CHAPTER ELEVEN
Cole

THE PLANE TOUCHED DOWN early Thursday morning, and the Marines cheered *oohrah* to be back on American soil. After a day of formation, a much-needed, not-to-hot shower (Cole had enough hot water to last a lifetime), and processing his furlough papers, he was free by Thursday afternoon. He didn't have to report back until Monday morning.

Three days of freedom.

Most of his squad wanted to see family or hit the bars, but Cole begged off.

He checked his phone again. It had been in his locked footlocker here on base, and Nowak had already texted him Isis's phone number.

Damn, that boy got in contact with the friend right quick.

Cole closed his footlocker and started to call, then paused with his thumb hovering over the send button. Calling was so old school, and he hadn't spoken to her for months.

Get it together, Maxton!

He swiped his thumb over his text app and typed in the number. Then he paused again.

What the fuck was he supposed to say? Hi, I haven't seen you in eight months, but I'm back. Wanna hang?

Stupid.

The sounds of Marines chatting and laughing in the hall startled him, and he tucked the phone to his side.

What the fuck? What was he, ten? Hiding the phone from a teacher?

Get it together, Cole!

Running his right hand through his still-wet, close-cropped curls, he started tapping with the tip of his thumb.

– Hey Isis! This is Cole. Remember me from the motel? I know it's been eight months and we said no strings, but I was wondering if you'd want to hang out again?

How long until she might text back? If she wanted to see him, maybe right away. If not . . .

He closed the app and tossed the phone onto his bed.

Better not to think about her if not . . .

Determined not to let the uncertainty get to him, he grabbed his duffel back and began sorting. Everything had to go to the laundry, and maybe he would go to the bar if he didn't hear back.

After everything was in order and clothes in the laundry, Cole grabbed the phone again.

Nothing.

It had been hours.

Wouldn't she have texted? Even if just to say *no thanks*?

He tapped the phone.

Maybe one more text to let her know it was okay to let him down.

– But if you meant the no-strings thing, please shoot me a quick message and I'll bug off.

There. That sounded nice enough, not too stalker-ish, and let her know he was good either way.

Yet he wasn't. He wanted her to call him back – hell, he longed for it, but if she was done, then he'd accept her choice.

But let me know so I have an idea of how drunk I'm getting tonight.

Dax Cameron stuck his head in the barracks room.

"Hey, man. We're heading to the bar, some upscale place this time. No dive bar and no fights. You comin' or not?"

Cole glanced down at his black t-shirt and dark blue jeans. Then he flicked his eyes down at his phone. Still nothing.

Fuck.

He turned to Dax and held his arms out to show off his plain black t-shirt. "This okay for an upscale place?"

Dax shrugged. "How do I know? Anything other than BDUs is fancy for me." Then his eyebrow rose when he noted the phone in Cole's hand. "Any luck with your mystery lady?"

While a snarky comment rose to Cole's tongue, Dax's question was earnest, so he shook his head.

"Well, she might be busy. Working. Out with friends. In the shower. Dead battery. She'll get back to you."

Cole stood and shoved the phone in his pocket as he joined Dax.

"Yeah."

But Cole wasn't as certain.

***

Dax, David, a few privates, and even Sergeant Beau Drake came along and encouraged Cole to join them. Sarge had sage advice that finally convinced him to get off his ass.

"She's just busy. Or your number is popping up as an unknown number, and she doesn't want to deal with it right now. Give her a day or so before you jump to the conclusion she's ghosting you."

As much as Cole hated to admit it, Sarge's words made complete sense.

Of course, she wouldn't recognize the number. He never looked at strange texts right away.

He ended up joining his men and reclining on a wobbly chair in the supposedly upscale bar. What else was he going to do – sit in the barracks all night while on furlough and mope?

Hell no.

At the bar though, his tough exterior came down hard, making him standoffish and reticent as he watched his squad drink and chat up every woman who entered the bar.

Nothing more sex-crazed than a Marine fresh off duty.

Look where it got you, something in the back of his mind said.

Shut it!

He pounded the last swig of his beer and pushed his long frame out of the chair to head to the bar for another. Sergeant Drake was leaning against the bar counter, his cowboy hat askew on his head.

It was always easy to tell where Sarge was when they were off duty or on leave or furlough. He wasn't as tall as Cole or Dax, but his light brown straw cowboy hat, the one Sgt. Drake called his Cattleman's hat, made him stand out anywhere.

Drake tilted his head a bit when Cole stepped next to him and rested his elbows on the edge of the bar. His hazel eyes burned like fire under his hat brim.

"So this woman, she has you twisted in circles?"

Cole lifted his beer bottle to the bartender as a way to ask for another and let his gaze drift back to his squad. Most of them at least. A few privates had left to meet up with family, but more than half sat with Dax and David, celebrating cooler air, cold water and beer, and no BDUs.

Drake twisted toward him and threaded his fingers together in front of his chest.

"Everyone knows the rumors. Hell, I saw you on your walk of shame back to the barracks the day before we deployed, and Nowak hasn't shut up about getting her number for you, which tells me several things."

Fuck.

Sgt. Drake was far too clever for the Marines. It was one reason he had already made sergeant. The man had a wicked-sharp mind.

Cole looked down at the beer bottle the bartender set in front of him and kept quiet.

"One, that you had a good enough time with this person to come back only minutes before Reveille. Two, for some reason, you didn't get her number, which is odd for this day and age. And she didn't give it to you herself, which is also odd. And three, she's not calling or texting you back the minute you got back from deployment. That tells me something else is going on. What has Iron Maxton twisted this way?"

Cole pursed his lips and twirled his beer bottle with his fingers. Drake had practically guessed, so there was no use keeping anything hidden. And Sarge wouldn't tell anyone else. His mind, and his mouth, were steel traps.

"I met her at the dive bar near base. Neither of us wanted anything, like no obligations or anything, and so we hooked up. It was supposed to be a one-night stand . . ."

He let the words fall off, and Sgt. Drake nodded. More than one Marine had intended to have a one-night stand and ended up married or with a pack of kids.

"No obligations. Like no phone numbers even?" Drake's eyebrows disappeared under his hat with his question.

"Yeah, that was just stupid on my part. By the time she dropped me off, things were good enough that I could have asked. My brain though . . . "

"Nowak got her number for you." Drake pointed vaguely to the Marines' table. "So what happened? You called her?"

"Texted," Cole corrected and sipped his beer. "But we had an agreement."

Drake huffed out a chuckle. "An agreement?"

Cole cut a quick glance at his sergeant, then refocused on his beer.

"Yeah. No strings, no relationship, no contact. One night only."

Drake's lips thinned into a smile, and he returned to his own drink on the bar.

"You know what they often call Marines who make that kind of agreement?"

Cole shook his head.

Drake gave him a sidelong grin. "The groom."

Chapter Twelve
Cole

The next morning, Cole fell back asleep after Reveille and didn't open his eyes until nearly nine. That was sleeping in for him, and he hadn't even stayed out late with his squad the night before. But it was such a comfort to sleep in a slightly softer bed, in a cool room, and not have to constantly think about waking from a poor sleep to grab his weapon.

Sleeping in the Marine barracks had some advantages.

The first thing he did once his mind fully woke was check his phone. Nothing.

Shower, shaved, and dressed, and checked his messages again. Nothing.

Fuck.

At this point, he was done with texts. Time to step up his game. Marines weren't known for being freaking coy, after all.

He stepped outside to a bench at the far end of the parking lot for a bit of privacy. The sun was hazy – springtime in Southern California near the beach was known for its gray mornings and sunny afternoons. The fresh air invigorated him, and he folded his long body on the bench, letting her number dial.

As it rang, he had a brief moment of alarm that the girl from the bar had given Nowak the wrong number, and he thought it was confirmed when a man answered the phone.

A very *angry*-sounding man.

"Who is this?"

Not the way to answer a phone call, but *okay* . . . He cleared his throat.

"Hello, sir. My name is Cole and I'm looking for Isis. Is she there?"

"Cole. You said your name is Cole?"

"Umm, yes, sir. Is Isis there?"

"You have some nerve calling her," the man growled.

What?

Through the phone, he heard some noise in the background. Then the phone call abruptly ended.

Stupefied, Cole stared at the cell phone in his hand.

What was *that* all about?

At first, it seemed that maybe he did have the wrong number. But the comment about having the nerve to call her meant that this angry man did know Isis. A new boyfriend? An old one who was jealous of his intimacy with Isis?

Iron Maxton wasn't one to back down from any fight. Clenching his jaw, he tried again.

The phone picked up on the first ring.

"Why are you calling her?" the angry voice bit out.

"Please, sir. I just got back from deployment. I met Isis before I left, and she was kind to me, and I just –"

Just what? He was rambling and he knew it. If she had a boyfriend, why the hell was Cole calling?

Sarge was right. Cole was twisted over this whole Isis thing.

He should have let it go.

But he wasn't one to live with regrets, so he'd never forgive himself if he didn't at least try to reach out — angry boyfriend or not.

Then again, if this man was *this* angry, maybe Isis wasn't in a great situation.

A snap of concern shot through Cole as he bolted up straight. His entire body shifted, hardened, and he refocused on what was important.

Making sure Isis was okay, no matter what else might be going on.

"I just wanted to make sure that she was good and let her know I got back safe."

"Good? Good? What the fuck –?"

With a sinking sensation in his chest, Cole pulled the phone from his ear. Something was going on. He was now on full alert.

Placing the phone back to his ear, he heard some scuffling through the earpiece, and then a woman's voice came on. Not Isis.

"Hello. You said your name is Cole?"

"Yes, ma'am."

The woman was silent for a second. "I think you need to see Isis."

More sounds in the background of the phone, but Cole barely registered it. That sentence didn't make any sense. And why didn't Isis get on the phone and speak to him? Was something wrong with Isis? Was she sick? In the hospital? In a car accident?

But if that was the case, why was the man so furious with him?

"Yeah, I'm on furlough for the next few days. I can do that. Are we meeting somewhere?"

More sounds in the background, then the woman spoke again.

"You can come here. I'll text you the address."

Come here? Where was here?

"Yes, ma'am. When should I show up?"

More background talk.

"Around lunchtime today. That should be good. Can you do that?" The woman's voice had lightened, almost conversational, a welcome change from the outraged man.

"Yes, ma'am. I'll be there at noon."

Click.

She hung up.

Maybe not as conversational as he'd thought.

His mind was as twisted as the rest of him after that phone call.

What the hell was going on?

Cole

The Uber drive to the house address was quick, as the house address wasn't too far from base.

Cole had let his sergeant know where he was going – always best to have a Marine's squad know their 10-14 – and after putting on a nicer shirt, a button down, he headed to the house a few miles south of Pendleton.

Knowing a Marine's 10-14, their location, was just one of the ways that the Marines made sure a squad, those who had his six, was able to do that. It was one of their primary training lessons.

As a Marine, he had to work as part of a team, a squad that relied on him as much as he relied on them. It worked both ways, and while the policy rubbed some Marines the wrong way, the best Marines realized they had to let their team back them as much as they did their duty to protect and support their team.

And with Sarge and the rest of his squad having his six, Cole grew more confident as the Uber driver turned onto the street.

Which was good, because he sure as hell wasn't confident about anything else that was about to happen.

Especially for a Marine, surprises were never a good thing.

Chapter Thirteen
Cole

Cole tapped the app on his phone to pay for the driver, exited the car, and stood at the end of the walkway as the car pulled away. He brushed his hands over his chest and stomach to smooth his shirt, ran his hands through the tight curls at the top of his head, and took a deep breath.

He tried to make sure he was prepared for anything that might happen when the front door opened.

How surprising that his Marine training should kick in while trying to visit a woman, one he knew and had met before. Hell, had slept with before.

Again the thought traversed his mind: *What the hell is going on?*

The house was on the larger size, two-story, with a two-car garage and small patio off the cream-colored front door. The entire house was stuccoed in shades of beiges and browns with windows (*possible points of egress,* his mind unconsciously noted) across the front. The entire house was unassuming enough in a decent-looking neighborhood.

Pulling his shoulders back, Cole marched up to the door and rang the doorbell, then took a long step back. Bracing himself.

The door whipped open and a middle-aged man, a few inches shorter than himself with a broad chest, filled the doorway.

"Are you Cole?" The man's voice was sharp.

Wow. No hello. No welcome.

Cole dipped his chin. "Yes, sir. Is Isis here?"

The man's already red face reddened more.

"Really. You want to talk to her now?"

"Chaz. I said to behave!" another voice called out.

An attractive blonde woman, presumably Chaz's wife, appeared in the doorway, shoving the fuming man to the side. Cole could do nothing but stare wide-eyed at the scene.

What was going on here? And where was Isis?

"I apologize for my husband. He's a nice guy but his temper can get the better of him at times."

"Sonia –" the man growled and the woman, Sonia, cut a hushing glare to him.

He hushed.

"I'm sorry, ma'am," Cole said as he tried to gather his wits. Give him a battle with an enemy over this odd, confusing mess anytime. "I thought Isis would be here."

Sonia looked him up and down with obvious scrutiny. "So you were deployed. Where?"

"Bahrain. I have embassy duty there, or I did. My squad is stationed at Pendleton for the meantime. I just got back yesterday."

Her lips pursed slightly. "Yesterday. And you texted her right away. That's something." She flicked her eyes at her frowning husband.

Cole tensed forward slightly. "I'm sorry. I think I'm missing something. I was deployed for eight months and didn't have any contact information for Isis or any way to get ahold of her. I texted as soon as wheels hit the tarmac. Can someone tell me what is going on? Is Isis okay?"

Then another voice carried past the couple to Cole.

"Mom, Dad. Come on. I told you it's fine. Don't be like this."

Isis's voice.

A warm rush of relief washed over him.

Fuck, he'd never been so glad to hear another person's voice in his life.

"Isis?" he asked.

He saw her face, her soft face with her ferocious celadon eyes and bright hair, coming down the darkened hallway.

Her parents stepped sideways to allow her access to the door, and that's when his eyes moved lower and dropped to her belly.

Her very *pregnant* belly.

Cole froze in place.

Isis was pregnant.

Chapter Fourteen
Isis

Seven months earlier.

Isis told herself over and over that she had taken her birth control pill in plenty of time.

That was the lie she told herself as she counted the days on her phone calendar again.

Maybe she had the dates wrong. Maybe it was stress – sometimes her period came late because of stress.

But she was lying to herself. Outright *lying* and she knew it.

Because it hadn't been one pill she'd missed. She had been slacking off a bit after her breakup, and work had been busy, and well, with stress and everything else, she had just forgotten.

When she had opened the packet after getting home from dropping off Cole, she went right to her pills.

Seven. She was off by *seven* days.

Oh, fuck me.

She took a pill right away, and then kept taking them. That was supposed to work, right? She was supposed to take a pill as soon as she realized she'd forgotten, which is what she had done.

And promptly forgot she had forgotten. After that pill, she was back on track.

Well, not fully. She had also lied to herself about being back on track – about the one-night stand which was the event she *was* supposed to forget.

Isis had found herself thinking about Cole at the most random times. When her friends joked about hanging out and drinking with the Marines, or Carly commented she had gotten the number of one of them. When the sky shifted into that impossible color of blue, like something from a fantasy movie, and was the exact shade of Cole's eyes.

Now one month later, and here she was, staring at an impossible calendar. Disbelieving, she counted the days again.

Two weeks late?

That was impossible. Impossible.

She had never been more than a day or two late since she'd started taking the pills.

Nononononono...

Isis grabbed her keys and her purse and raced for her car. A drugstore was just down the street from her apartment, and she hurried in, bought the smooth white package, and then rushed back home.

Everything felt rushed, as if life suddenly had a timer, one that ticked loudly in the back of her mind, counting down the seconds to its inevitable end.

Tick tock...

Isis went directly to the bathroom that she shared with her roommate, who fortunately was not home. They had moved in together the year before, but that roomie relationship had started to deteriorate since her roomie had gotten serious with her boyfriend. Isis hadn't missed the hints that the roomie would like for Isis to move out so Brenda could move her boyfriend in.

She locked the bathroom door and tore open the package.

Tick tock...

Following the instructions, Isis then set the stick on the counter and waited.

So much waiting.

Tick tock . . .

She forced herself to wait the excruciatingly long three minutes, flipping through insipid videos on her phone. The idea of reading on her book app to read was out of the question. Her mind was wild.

Tick tock . . .

Her phone dinged and she took a deep breath, then rose from her seat on the closed toilet and looked down at the stick.

Two purple lines.

Two.

She lifted the stick and stared at it.

No! How?

One night.

The first time in weeks, no – months – that she'd been with a guy!

And because she's forgotten her pill . . . but holy hell – one night?

What did they feed Marines?

Isis set the stick aside and gripped the edge of the sink. Her vision grayed and her knees felt like sponges, weak and shifty. It was hard to breathe in the closed bathroom. She sank back down onto the toilet seat.

And she couldn't even tell Cole or let him know, because he was in another freaking country, and she never got his number.

She knew his name, Cole Maxton. Corporal Cole Maxton.

And that was about all she knew.

She didn't even know where he was exactly or when he was getting back to the US.

Dropping her head into her hands, Isis took several deep breaths.

Oh. My. God.

So much for no strings attached.

She was pregnant.
Tick tock . . .

Chapter Fifteen
Isis

It took Isis several days to get control of her raging emotions. She kept zoning out – more than once, another librarian or a patron had to work to get her attention, or her mother, who had started to look at her sideways. That wise woman knew something was going on, but Isis was sure she'd not guess what it was.

Her mother would be excited to be a grandmother. Her father . . . she sighed heavily. Well, that was another story.

Isis sat at the dinner table two weeks after she had taken that fateful pregnancy test. Her mother had invited her over for Saturday grilling on the back deck, and though it was autumn, it was autumn in southern California, so it was seasonally warm.

She had shared the news only with Carly and Deidre. It turned out Carly had the number of one of the guys, and offered to give it to her, but the guy had said they wouldn't have their phones back until they returned next year.

Next year!

Isis's stomach dropped to her feet.

And Carly, being the voice of reason, urged her to tell her parents and start planning. Either to keep it or take care of the situation. But make up her mind fast and tell her parents if she was keeping the baby.

The baby.

More swirling in her mind. Every thought was so elusive; as soon as she thought she might hold onto one, it slipped by and returned to the swirling mass.

Tick tock...

After some soul searching, she decided to keep the baby. At first, it seemed like a crazy decision, but then she realized it was not. It wasn't like she was a young teenager or without a job. She had a college degree and an excellent position at the library with benefits. Getting her own place would to be a struggle on her salary, but she'd find something.

Isis had wanted a relationship that was more real, more substantial, and if that relationship wasn't a child, she didn't know what it was.

And this baby was created in a moment that was perfection with Cole – a moment she'd never experienced ever in her life. This shocking turn of events came from such a good place. Even if he wasn't around to be a daddy, her father would be an amazing grandfather, and she'd have her mother's help. And Carly and Deidre.

Yeah, this baby was a *good* thing. A wonderful reminder of that night with Cole.

Once that decision was made, it was time to inform her parents. Several times throughout dinner, Sonia paused and asked Isis what was on her mind.

She knows...

She *had* to. Wasn't that a saying? That mothers just know?

Chaz, short for the unfortunate name Chester, set his fork and knife down and swiveled his head from Isis to his wife.

"Is there something I'm missing?" he asked with a slight smile on his broad face.

Sonia lifted her chin toward Isis and narrowed her hazel eyes slightly. Isis had gotten her gray-green eye coloring from her father.

"I think Isis has something to tell us. You've seemed distracted tonight."

Here we go...

"I am. I have some news, and I'm not sure how you're going to take it."

Her dad stiffened, but her mother gave her a warm smile, a motherly smile, and reached over to pat her hand.

"We're okay with hearing anything you need to tell us, sweetheart."

Isis's mouth opened and closed several times – how hard was it to form the two simple words?

Not so simple.

Isis picked at the seam of her jeans. She couldn't look at them while she said it.

"So it turns out I'm pregnant. You're going to be grandparents."

The words came out in a breathless rush, and she kept her gaze lowered.

Quiet shock hung over the table. Then her mother clapped. "Oh, Isis! What amazing news!"

Her dad was quiet. Isis glanced at him, then back at her mother.

"Are you excited?" Her mother's question held a lot more implication than if Isis was excited.

But she *was* excited. Scared, overwhelmed, and excited.

Tick tock...

Isis finally smiled. "Yeah, I am. It's a surprise, but I'm in a good place so I think –"

"You're in a good place?" her father barked. "You're not married, you don't even have a boyfriend, and you don't make shit working for the library. Oh my god." Her father's face darkened. "This isn't Darren's is it? That asshole. Did he do this to you?"

Sonia cut Chaz a challenging look while Isis gritted her teeth. "No, Dad. Not Darren. And no one *did* this to me. I was a part of it, and I made this decision."

Chaz leaned his elbow on the table. "Who did this, then? How did this happen?"

"Chaz!" Sonia chastised.

Isis silently thanked her mother.

She couldn't believe her dad was asking that, but she knew what he meant.

And only Carly and Deidre knew about Cole.

Sonia looked at Isis, her eyes kind but her jaw set.

"Sweetheart, have we met the father? Can you tell us what's going on?"

How could she tell them about Cole when she barely knew more about him than his name and that he was a now-deployed Marine? She'd have to hedge.

Isis cleared her throat.

"So, he's a Marine. I met him a few months ago. We hit it off, but he deployed and here I am."

Isis saw her mom's lips twitch. Fortunately, that was her only negative reaction.

"Have you been able to talk to him about it? I mean, I see on TV that those military guys get screen time or something . . . "

Her mother knew even less about the Marines or military life than she did.

"No. I wasn't dating him, really. And now he's deployed and I don't get to talk to him, so . . ."

"So he doesn't know," Chaz grumbled in his tight voice.

He was biting back anger, and other than not being married, Isis didn't know why his reaction was so harsh. She was an adult, a college graduate, with a full-time job. Women like her had babies all the time, baby-daddy in the picture or not.

"No, Dad. He doesn't know."

"This random guy knocks up my daughter and then leaves the country. That's what you are saying to me."

"Chaz!"

"Dad!"

"Sonia!" Chaz turned on his wife. "I don't care if I sound like a caveman or something! This is *my* daughter! And some guy puts her in this situation and bails? And I'm the bad guy?"

Tears burned in her eyes, and Isis shoved her chair back to get up and leave. To escape. Her mother, however, acted quickly, stood up, and held her hand out to Isis and she sat back down.

Sonia then turned her force of will on her husband.

"That's enough, Chaz. She has enough on her plate without you adding to it. If she's happy about this, then we're happy about this. And if the father is a part of it, then fine. If not, then fine. And you'll be okay with it and be the happiest grandpa on the planet."

Sonia's words had bite. Isis blinked hard, unable to look away from her mother. Knowing her mother was on her side, ready to fight battles for her, lifted a gigantic weight from her shoulders.

Her father's face went through a series of expressions before he sank back in his chair.

"Okay. Okay. I'm not happy about the father situation. I'd like to have that figured out eventually. He does have obligations here, but if you're happy, sweetheart," Chaz said as he turned his deep-set gray-green eyes to her, "then I'm happy for you. And I will be everything that baby needs."

A tiny smile played on Sonia's lips, and this time Isis did rise. She walked over to her father and standing behind him, she hugged his wide shoulders.

"Thank you, Dad," she said in a low voice.

"But I will meet this guy as soon as he's back. You got that?"

Isis shared a quick look with her mother, who shrugged. She could only do so much.

"I got that."

Chapter Sixteen
Cole

Cole couldn't take his eyes off Isis and her round belly. It looked like someone shoved a basketball under her light green shirt, and he couldn't tear his eyes away. It was like someone sucker punched him and he was struggling to recover.

"Well, come on in, then," Sonia said and moved to the side.

"Cole?" Isis asked, snapping him back to attention. "You want to come in?"

He blinked rapidly. "Yeah. I mean, yes, ma'am."

He looked from Sonia to the man, Chaz, then stepped over the threshold.

Isis is pregnant?

And . . . it's mine? It has to be with they way her father is acting . . .

That's what he had to presume. Otherwise, she would have texted him back and said don't bother, and her father wouldn't look like he was ready to tear his head off.

Cole opened his mouth to ask about it, but no words came out. His brain had completely shut down like an overheated Humvee.

Isis glanced down at herself, then lifted those stunning misty green eyes to him.

"I'm sorry you had to find out this way," she said.

"Don't apologize to him!" her dad barked from behind him.

The man closed the front door, and it was as if he had sealed Cole's fate.

Cole couldn't understand a single thing that was going on, and here he was with this irate father breathing down his neck.

"Don't apologize to him! He should apologize to you," Chaz growled.

Cole's neck twitched as Sonia moved closer to her husband.

"Chaz! Now is not the time. I told you to behave."

The dad quieted, but Cole swore he could hear the fury burning off the man in waves.

He couldn't let the mom rush to his defense like that. He was a Marine corporal! He could defend himself. And he understood why the man was angry. Cole didn't blame him at all.

"It's okay," he said aloud to everyone. "I'm a responsible person. I'm in the military, for fu — for goodness sake. I'm all about accountability." Then he shifted toward Isis. "I just need to know what's going on."

Her face softened as she gazed at him. She looked different but still as beautiful as he remembered. Her head moved and she looked at her mother.

"Mom?"

Sonia nodded. "It's such a nice spring day. Why don't you two sit outside? I'll bring snacks and water."

A wash of relief passed over Isis's face, and she tilted her head toward the hall.

"Follow me?"

Isis's voice was barely above a whisper, and it only made Cole's heart ache even more. *Fuck,* how he had missed her. Even in all this chaos, his heart ached for her.

Isis's statement was more of a question, but what else was he going to do? Say no? Not follow her?

No sir. That wasn't an option.

Her walk was more of a waddle as she led him down the hall, and he had to force himself not to grin as he followed.

Despite the pure and absolute shock of the moment, seeing her face, her funny walk, just being in her presence, steeled him for this conversation.

He had waited eight months to see her again and had thought about her constantly while he was in country. He wasn't about to let this newly discovered situation become an issue or take away his joy at seeing her. He'd do everything to show her he was on board, whatever *that* entailed. Yet the shock of it all held him in an iron grip.

They sat at a lovely patio set in the well-landscaped backyard. He pulled out her chair, and she sat heavily, holding her ample belly with one hand. Cole took the chair right next to her.

He twisted and rested his elbow on his knees so his face was close to hers. He wanted to do everything to show that he was there. *Present*, as he'd heard his lieutenant say once.

"Are you okay?" he asked, his voice shaking.

Cole might put on a brave face, but he certainly was not ready for this conversation. Hell, who ever was?

Isis looked up and caught Cole's eyes. For a moment, neither of them spoke. So much needed to be said between them, but it was the most difficult thing he had to do, keeping that eye contact while waiting for her response. This made basic training look like child's play.

Isis finally nodded. "Yeah, I'm good. I didn't really want to tell you like this."

In a moment of impetuous bravery, he reached out and clasped her hand. Her nails were painted a dark pink, and he held her hand tight. He had to ask a few hard questions and presumably was going to hear a few rough answers. Better to be grounded together than free-falling apart.

He had her six, after all.

Sonia came out with a tray of fruit and cups of sparkling water. She gave Cole a kind smile and then left quickly. Cole appreciated her candor.

"Were you going to tell me at all?" His voice was thick with emotion.

Isis licked her lips. "Honestly, I wasn't sure. I didn't even have your number, and you were out of the country."

Fair.

"And it was a no-strings-attached night. No obligations. So I wasn't sure if I was going to tell you because of that."

Again fair, but that knowledge stabbed a knife in his heart. He had intended to see if she wanted strings when he returned, and now here those strings were, forced on them.

"Yeah, well, life shifted quickly, then," he admitted.

Isis nodded and pursed her lips.

"I was still going to try and find you after I got back. I haven't been able to stop thinking about you. This," he gestured with his hand, "changes things, but only a little bit."

Her hand stiffened in his.

"What?" she asked.

"That night together, hell, Isis. The memory of it, of you, got me through this most recent deployment. I told myself that if one night with this woman can do that for me, then maybe it does need strings and obligations. I need someone like that in my life. You need to know that about me, Isis."

He paused and leaned in closer, the heat between them building. "I'm a Marine, and I take that duty seriously. I'm all about protection, about duty. I'm about standing up and doing the right thing. There's no way I would walk away, no matter how difficult or shocking the obligations might be. This development just means I need to take those strings more seriously."

Her gaze dropped briefly before rising to meet his again. "I appreciate that, but you don't have to do anything. And if you had these dreams of some passionate relationship with me, I think this changes that idea. And I had already decided I was going to be okay as a single mom. My dad might hate it, but I was okay with it from the get-go. You don't have to do anything."

Was she trying to push him away, or was something else going on? Cole wasn't about to let their previous agreement live on when everything had changed, though he understood she might not be of a mind for any relationship right now. She had other worries than if they would date or not.

But he would do anything and everything for her. He'd give all, and whatever she could give, he'd accept.

Cole shook his head. "No, that's not right. I don't want you to be a single mom. That's a big burden, and I can do a lot. I want to be there, be a big part, be a dad, do everything I can. I can get you resources and stuff from the military. Medical care, a dependent pass, housing, all that. I know we have a lot to talk about, but let's get that set up for you and the baby to start. I can do that right away."

He really didn't know what else he would be doing until after the baby was born, and even then . . . What? Feed the baby? Change diapers? It didn't matter.

He was all in.

And he'd figure out a way to show her.

Isis smiled. "Thank you. I really appreciate that offer. You didn't sign up for this. We had agreed to no obligations, and I am sorry that this happened and changed all that."

He lifted her hand and kissed it. "*Improvise. Overcome. Adapt.* That's a Marine saying. We train on that philosophy because a good Marine knows that nothing ever goes according to plan. So if there's one thing I know, it's that even the best plans can shift on a dime, and I never want to think of this baby as a mistake or something I didn't want. This is just a shift, a change, and the Marines have taught me how to improvise under any circumstance."

They were quiet for a moment, then she reached across and took his other hand in a light grip.

It wasn't much, but it was something. Cole's heart trembled in his chest.

"Not quite the welcome home you expected, eh?" she said with a wry smile.

There was that smile he'd keep in his mind while he was gone.

Cole grinned back. "No, I can't imagine a bigger surprise. My head is still spinning."

"My dad pushed the issue. I was going to wait a bit longer, let you be home for a bit, but when you texted, my dad went ballistic. I just wanted this to be easy for you."

A muscle in his jaw twitched. "Nope. Don't do that. Don't try to make anything easy for me. I don't think this is going to be easy for you at all, and it's my job to step up and try to remove as much of that weight from you as I can. And I will do anything and everything to make that possible."

Talking to her, even discussing this unexpected development, put him at ease. What was it about her that calmed him even under the most distressing moments? Most other men would have fallen apart at a surprise like this. Being with Isis made him feel that anything was possible.

"Can I ask how this all happened? I thought we, or you at least, were covered?"

A stupid question. And he knew better than to put the onus of safe sex on her – he should have worn a condom. The Marines beat *that* directive into their heads so much it should have been as natural as checking his surroundings on a mission. They even had coded terminology for it – *safety brief, holster your gun, guard your bridge . . .* So this was as much his fault, if not more, than hers. But he was curious as to what happened.

"I was on the pill. But after my breakup, I kept forgetting to take the pills, but I wasn't with anyone, so it wasn't a huge issue. All it takes is missing one dose."

His mouth popped open. "I didn't know that!"

Isis shrugged, and he understood the gesture. *It is what it is.*

He had a sudden thought. "Okay, so what can I do now? Do you have doctor's appointments? I can take you. Are there medical bills that I need to help pay for? Do you need things for the baby? I can help with all that. I *need* to help with all that."

Something in her face shifted, and she ran her hand over her baby bump. The gesture made his insides quiver.

"Thank you. That makes me feel better. I won't lie, Cole, I have been worried about all of this. Telling you about the baby topped that list of worries. I was debating if I was going to tell you at all. Now that you know, the rest seems easier. At least until the baby's born." Her smile widened a bit, and it made her entire face light up.

Christ, he could stare at the smile for the rest of his life.

God willing, that was what would happen. He'd do everything in his power to make that happen.

"I was going to go shopping this weekend," she said to him. "I moved back in with my parents as I got everything figured out, and we're getting a nursery set up in a spare bedroom upstairs. Do you want to see it?"

His heart raced at the invitation, then he paused and gape at her. *Nursery? Decorating?*

It felt like he stepped off a cliff and was free-falling.

Then his breath stuck in his throat at his next thought. Cole swallowed hard and tried not to clamp down on her hands.

"Do you know what it is? The gender?" he asked in a wavering tone.

The smile she gave him was unlike anything he had ever seen before. One of care and tenderness and understanding, and his heart completely melted in his chest.

"It's a girl."

All the air in his lungs evaporated, and he was breathless.
A daughter.
A little girl of all his own. A little girl to spoil and protect and have tea parties and dances but also to teach how to shoot.

It was like a whole new world had opened up, and Cole never imagined the pure surge of joy that could suffuse through him as it did in that moment with Isis.

He swallowed the hard lump of emotion in his throat and released her hand to run his fingers through his tight curls at the crown of his head.

"I'd love to see the nursery."

Chapter Seventeen
Isis

Isis rose, still in a state of utter shock. Carly had told her one of the Marines from the bar had her number and texted her a few times, and that in one of those texts, he had asked for Isis's number. Carly had handed it over without question and let Isis know after the fact. Though Isis had put on a tough exterior, she was secretly glad that Carly had done so.

But she still didn't believe it would amount to anything. Why would any guy take on this burden if he could just bail?

Now Cole was here, in front of her, in all his tall, fit, blue-eyed glory. She had told him about her impending baby, and he had taken it in stride. Who did that? How did he simply accept that this was their new reality when it had taken her weeks – no, months – to get used to it? And sometimes it still caught her by surprise.

Worse than all that was her visceral, physical reaction to him. Though she had written him off – heck she didn't even have his number! – a small part of her had hoped she might see him again. That fate might somehow lend its improbable hand and lead her back to her proverbial door.

She had thought she might faint when her dad opened the door, and he was there. In the flesh, his tall frame, straight back, and close-cut curls on top of his head, and she still didn't quite believe it was him. Even though her father had answered the call (*and oh, the fight they'd had over that one!*) and her mother invited him over, Isis still didn't fully imagine he would show up.

Fate just didn't happen create miracles like it did in the story books Isis read to children at the library. Fate in the real world could be a cruel mistress, so until Cole spoke, until he expressed any interest in the baby at all, she suspended her belief.

But here he was. Real. Touching her. His earnest eyes studying her face as his warm, long-fingered hand held hers. She had a flash as they sat outside – would their baby have his same long fingers? His intense eyes? Those brown curls that made him look so much younger than his mid-twenties?

And then when he said that their night together got him through his deployment…

Had her heart ever wrenched so hard in her life? Her body ever been so breathless?

To know that his thoughts had been on her as her mind had been on him?

Though his words robbed her body of breath, she tamped down her primitive reaction to them. Things were different now. This meeting wasn't the opportunity to have more free nights together; she had a new focus, which threw a wrench into everything.

As they spoke, she realized that she might have lost a thrilling opportunity for love, but she found, at least it seemed for the moment, a chance for Cole to be a good father and an involved co-parent.

That was more than she could have hoped for.

And if that was all they would ever be, then she'd take it and be grateful. So many people had much less.

Isis rose awkwardly, and Cole rushed to her side, his tall, muscled form making her heart flutter at his nearness. Then, when he rested his hand on her upper back, his touch made her quiver.

"Here. Do you need help up?"

The concern in his voice only added to her twitter-pated state.

"No, I'm okay," she said as she pushed her body up with the help of the table.

How was she going to keep her emotions in check if he was this attentive? Maybe this was going to be too much for her.

She glanced at him and tipped her head toward the house.

"It's upstairs. Come on."

The carpeted stairs led to a hallway at the top, separating the upstairs into two sections – the main bedroom with a fully attached bath and walk-in closet to the right, and the three smaller bedrooms to the left. The guest bath was immediately off the stairwell. She led him to the smallest bedroom near the steps.

Her parents had insisted she move in once she told them about the baby. She had already griped about her roommate, and her mother had made the executive decision. Chaz was more than ready to go along – he hadn't loved the idea of his only child living with what he called a degenerate. Not the kindest term for Brenda, but at the time, Isis didn't care.

The prospect of a nice house in the suburbs with a proper nursery won out over stuffing the crib into her bedroom in a cheap, two-room apartment.

She and Sonia had begun decorating before they knew if the baby was a boy or a girl, so they started the decor with yellows and white, then added some pinks after the ultrasound. Isis didn't want too much girly stuff in the nursery, preferring a decor in the style of Peter Rabbit, with green and light blue accents. Isis stepped inside the room and turned to Cole. She needed to see his reaction.

Cole froze at the doorway. He was so tall he seemed to take up the entire space as he remained fixed, his eyes roving from place to place in the room, from the crib bedding to the light yellow and white striped walls to the Peter Rabbit wall art. His mouth popped open as he stared.

A hot flare of panic struck Isis in the chest.

Oh no.

Was this too much? Was he changing his mind?

He took one step onto the cream-colored carpet and paused again, his head rotating this way and that.

Please say something! she begged silently.

"This is stunning," he finally said in a halting tone.

"Thank you. My mom and I did most of it ourselves, with Dad painting. Peter Rabbit is one of my favorite stories." She swept her hand to the large bunny art around the room.

"The stories with Farmer McGregor?" he asked in an awe-filled voice.

Most of his attention was on the room, and she was mildly surprised he asked the question, let alone know anything about Peter Rabbit stories.

Isis licked her lips to hide her grin.

"Yeah, and we added a bit of pink after we knew –"

Her words ended abruptly as the baby moved hard in her belly, shoving hard with a foot. She released a heady breath and touched the spot where her impossible future made herself known.

Cole's eyes immediately lasered in on her.

"Are you okay?"

The awe in his voice had been replaced with concern, and the side of her mouth curled as she reached out for him.

"She's moving. Do you want to feel her?"

His expression returned to shock and awe. He might be a hardened Marine, but this baby news was hitting him hard, shattering that tough exterior. She had to force herself not to laugh at him.

He's still in shock over the news that he's going to be a dad! Give him a break, she told herself.

Cole didn't move, so she grabbed his hand and placed it atop her loose gray t-shirt. He was riveted, his eyes focused on his hand and her belly.

The baby was kind enough to reward her and shifted again, pressing in a moving curve up and under Cole's hand. He gasped as his eyebrows shot high on his forehead. His earnest eyes widened as large as dinner plates.

But Isis understood. That movement – it made all the words, all the conversation, real. This was more than an idea or upcoming event, something intangible. No. The baby was now nearly ready to make her appearance.

Tick tock . . .

"That's – that's her?" His voice was more like a squeak.

Absolutely comical for a Marine.

The baby wasn't even here yet, and she was wrapping this rough and ready man around her finger. He was going to be melted butter in this baby's hands.

Isis gave Cole a soft smile. "That's her. A foot, I think, as she wiggles. It's getting tight in there and I've noticed when I climb the stairs, she moves more. I think it squishes her a bit."

Cole didn't move his hand but waited to feel her again. This touch, being joined like this, was at once hypnotic and exhilarating, and it was made more so by the new life their one incredible night had created.

Isis kept her hand on his and shifted, trying to encourage the baby to react. The baby obliged, stirring again, lighter this time, and Cole's stunned expression transformed into a beaming smile.

"That's amazing."

He pulled his hand away, and it was like he pulled on her heart at the same time. She plastered a subdued look on her face and smoothed her t-shirt over her burgeoning belly.

He had moved closer to her, and again, she was overwhelmed by the ferocity of his nearness.

"Do you have a name yet?" he asked. His voice had shifted as well, his voice as subdued as she felt.

"Aurore. It's a variation of a Greek goddess. And Faye for the middle name. It's a family name on my mom's side."

"Aurore Faye. That's beautiful." The awe was back in his voice.

Then he was quiet, and they stood together in the nursery.

Is he waiting for something? Does he have another question?

Then his hand moved, lightly touching her bare upper arm and sliding down to take her hand.

Isis let out a shaky breath at his touch.

"I know this isn't anything we expected, and we have a lot to do and work on in the next few months. But none of that changes how I feel about you or how you make me feel when I'm with you. Since I don't know where we stand or what the future might hold, I'll keep my distance if that's what you want. I won't make a move unless you want me to. If you don't, if you want to keep this –" he waggled his finger back and forth between them, "platonic and focused only on the baby, then I'll accept that."

Then he leaned in, not much – just enough for the heat of his nearness to make her lightheaded.

"But when, or if, you want more, I'm ready to give it. I'm here for the baby, but I returned for you."

Isis's chest pounded under the throbbing of her heart. What woman didn't want to hear words like his?

However, the reality was that they barely knew each other, and she had more pressing issues on her plate. She wanted everything but was afraid of getting it.

Cole seemed to know that she was conflicted because he gave her hand a light squeeze, then gently released it and took a small step to the side. He returned his attention to the room, and Isis released a shaky breath.

"You seem to have everything. Is there anything you still need? I'm on furlough through tomorrow, then my current duties have me working on base during the week until six. And I'm going to start reaching out to Family Readiness as soon as I get back on base. But I can help get stuff, go shopping, diapers. . . Do you have any doctor visits that I need to go to? Please, anything you and the baby, Aurore, need."

There he was, Cole the Marine. After opening his chest to show her his heart, he wrapped it back up and was all business.

And as flustered as she was right now, Isis was happy he could compartmentalize like that.

Because *she* certainly couldn't.

"Do you want to go with me and pick up the last couple items? We already had a shower, so I have a good amount of things, but there are a few extras. Plus, a few unused gift cards. And I was, of course, going to stock up on more diapers. We could go shopping next weekend."

A shadow passed over his face, and her throat tightened. Was that suddenly too much for him?

"When are you due? How much time do we have to get ready for her?"

How much time do we have . . . his words were a salve on her heart.

"About four weeks."

"Four weeks," he repeated in that awe-inspired voice. Then he riveted his blue gaze back to her. He was in full Marine mode. "We'll be ready."

CHAPTER EIGHTEEN
Cole

LANCE CORPORAL DAX CAMERON caught up with Cole as he was striding back to the barracks. Cole had just left the Family Readiness office with a list of what he needed to get, how to put the baby on his benefits, and what he could do for Isis.

That was the worst part. The reason he didn't see Dax was that his mind was working hard, trying to figure out the best way to make all his benefits work for her. They weren't married, which put a stopper on most of what he could do for Isis directly.

And not for the first time since returning and learning about the baby, the idea of getting married crossed his mind. Marines tied the knot all the time when a girlfriend got pregnant, sometimes in less than a month after meeting the girlfriend in question. The Marine married the woman, had the baby, lived on base housing, and the Marine Corps took care of everything from medical care to food.

But he and Isis weren't married. And while he had known her for eight months now, the amount of time they had actually talked to or seen each other was far less than any of those one-month-and-married relationships.

Worse, he had shared his heart with her, yet she hadn't said anything in return to indicate she might care for him in any way, let alone the depth for which he cared for her.

Shit.

He had fallen for her hard – he had been smitten since their conversation outside the bar. And now that he was here, it seemed so much conspired against him.

No matter what, he had vowed to himself he would do everything to keep a good relationship with Isis and be a great dad, even if the romance fizzled. He wouldn't let her rejection of him taint this incredible moment he was certain he'd ever have.

Cole was not seen as the family-man type. Not Iron Maxton.

This little girl wasn't even in the world yet, and he melted every time he thought about her.

No matter what, he'd keep the baby at the center of his universe, even if his heart was trampled to pieces.

Those were his thoughts when a shouting voice broke through his tumultuous thoughts.

"Hey, Cole! Did you get a hold of that girl?"

That was a loaded question. But the news was going to get out sooner as opposed to later, and maybe Dax had some advice.

"Yeah. Yeah, I did."

Dax fell into stride next to him. "And? Does she want to see you again?"

Cole's jaw worked. "In a way. It turns out she's pregnant. Very pregnant."

Dax froze mid-step, and Cole had to turn around to face him. He tried to keep a level expression on his face. It wouldn't do to let his squad know he was simpering over a woman he'd met once and this baby.

"Pregnant?" Dax's face was a comical mask of shock. "Like how pregnant? And do you mean *you're* pregnant?"

The implications were rife in Dax's questions.

"Yeah. She's ready to burst. The timeline fits. It's mine."

Dax's face appeared dumbfounded. "How did that happen? Didn't you . . .?" His eyebrows lifted to finish the question.

"Failed birth control." That answered everything. Simple enough.

Dax nodded. "Okay. So your reunion didn't go as planned, I guess. What's going to happen now? Did you talk to the benefits people?"

He sounded genuinely sympathetic with a listening ear.

Cole glanced over his shoulder the way he had come. "Yeah. Just left there. I can get a lot of stuff for the baby, but since Isis and I aren't married . . ."

His own words drifted off, but Dax didn't need the rest. Every Marine understood that conundrum.

"The same thing happened to a guy I know in another squad. We were at basic together, and shortly after, his girl fell pregnant. No bennies for her until they got married."

Cole's curiosity was piqued. "How did that go?"

Dax shrugged one shoulder. "I dunno. The guy was young, and so was the girl. Probably not the best situation." He paused and sucked on his bottom lip briefly as he assessed Cole. "But he's not Iron Maxton. You're older, not a private, and your girl is not a girl. She's older, at least from what I've heard, with a real job, right?"

Cole nodded. "And a degree. She's educated. A librarian."

Dax whistled and gave Cole a sardonic grin. "Look at you, moving up in the world with your fancy girlfriend."

Cole's chin dropped, and Dax's gaze narrowed at him in a way that might make a lesser man shudder. For all his comedic traits, Dax had the gaze of a predatory falcon when he focused those oddly bright green eyes on someone. "What?"

"Not so much a girlfriend. Right now, we're just trying to maneuver this baby news."

"Right, right. And that's the difference between you and the private. You know what to focus on." Then Dax's face brightened, the predatory look gone, and he slapped Cole's shoulder. "But I saw how she had you turned upside down while we were in the desert. I know you have a charming side under that hard exterior. And if she's as smart as you say she is, she'll see it. I have a good feeling about this."

Dax slapped his shoulder again and headed into the barracks. "See you at mess!" he shouted.

Cole followed him slowly as he considered Dax's words.

Maybe she would see past his tough exterior. He had already lowered it so much around her as it was. Perhaps if he kept that hard edge down, she'd see who he really was and care for him as he cared for her.

God, he hated to admit Lance-Corporal Cameron might be right.

Chapter Nineteen
Isis

The week was a long one, especially for Isis as she tried to figure out what she was going to do with Cole and why she was feeling so dizzied over him and his reappearance in her life.

He texted her every day.

That alone was enough to throw her already off-kilter life into a tailspin. The attention he gave her alone was enough to make anyone swoon!

And not just about the baby. How was *she* doing? What was *her* favorite color? Why was Peter Rabbit *her* favorite? How long had *she* been a librarian?

He also told her about the military's benefits for the baby and her, by extension.

All those conversations that they should have had, all the conversations they didn't have on that one impossible night, he was trying to make up for now.

It was as if he was trying to make up for lost time, measuring out the moments they should have had with kind texts and soft words, with his intense eyes and warm hands, with their memories of a shared night and their hopes for the future, until the time they had lost was refilled.

And the prospect of Cole in her life both thrilled and unnerved her. What if they didn't work well as parents? What if something happened that made them hate each other?

Or worse, what if he was deployed again and never came back? He had said that thoughts of her kept him going in Bahrain, but thoughts and memories were nothing but weak veils, ineffective cover against an IED or rogue bullet.

That was a thought she didn't let take root in her mind. She'd not breathe that idea into existence and rob her daughter of the joy of a father before Aurore had the chance to know him.

And Cole did seem like a great guy.

But the other considerations – couples fell apart all the time. And she and Cole didn't have the strongest start to whatever their relationship might be.

He had also called every night after he was done with his duties and she finished her shift at the library. He always asked about her health and the baby, but then they chatted.

Simple, easy conversations.

Some nights it lasted hours.

Isis had known there was something about him that she craved, otherwise they never would have had that amazing night nearly a year ago. She had liked him when he left her car.

But to like him *this* much? To get to know him? To feel so comfortable with him, find him easy to talk to, even exciting to talk to? The confident timber of his voice and his funny anecdotes about the military, everything about him, only confused her more.

She started referring to her problematic, rising emotions as *the Cole situation.*

Problematic because she had a baby to focus on. Aurore needed her attention, not a mother distracted by a hot Marine.

Tick tock . . .

Nonetheless, his attention and his affectionate tone were nice to hear and a great way to pass the time.

For their shopping trip, they agreed to meet on Saturday morning, with Isis picking him up right outside base. They planned on hitting a few baby-oriented stores at a nearby shopping center before heading back to base, where he offered to take her shopping at the PX for anything she might need.

When she picked him up, Cole was stiff and structured, in full Marine mode.

It must be because he's on base, she presumed.

Once in the baby store, however, Cole's demeanor changed. He became absolutely giddy picking out clothes, holding pink, green, and yellow gowns and onesies against his chest as if he was going to wear them, holding up bottles to see which "felt" the best, and going full Marine mode when looking at strollers – the one significant item she still didn't own.

Cole took down several of the nearly industrial-sized strollers, checking how they opened and closed, how well the booster or car seat snapped in, and evaluating the features.

After each one, he gave a run down to Isis, along with pros and cons, cracking jokes the entire time. At one point, he was lying on his floor to see how the seat snapped in, and Isis lost it. She burst out laughing at his antics.

"What?" he asked, his eyes wide under his shock of brown curls.

"You! It's a stroller!"

He grinned, exposing a flash of white teeth, then sat up as he shifted his long legs.

"I know. I'm going overboard. But this is my first baby. Ever. No younger siblings, no little cousins. And this is our daughter. I want to make sure everything we do is as perfect as we can make it."

As perfect as we can make it.

Not perfect, and she loved that he acknowledged the obvious reality of life's imperfections.

But they could love the imperfections.

Why am I thinking like this? she questioned herself before refocusing on the task at hand.

Strollers.

"Well, are you okay with any of these three?"" Cole asked as he stood. He had three strollers that passed muster lined up in front of him.

Since she hadn't even looked at strollers, and he had investigated every square inch of them, she nodded.

"Of them, this one is the easiest for me to push. The bar is high, and it has good security features for the seat and wheels. But I won't be the only one pushing, so why don't you push them and see which one is best for you."

Isis moved to the first one and paused.

They pretty much all looked the same to her – other than shades of color and wheel size. She was shorter than him by more than a few inches, but why get a stroller that would make his back ache to push, when it made little difference to her? After pushing all three, she selected the one that was easier for him to push. Isis didn't have a preference overall, and better to encourage his paternal instincts.

Cole also grabbed onesies and a few colored gowns and even a pink and white frilly dress that came with a matching headband.

"Really?" Isis asked, eyeing the tiny dress. "Where are we going where she'll wear something that fancy?"

Cole's wide smile was infectious. He was like a kid in a candy store.

"Who knows? She can wear it to nap time for all I care. I just want to see her in it."

His pure exuberance was infectious, and not for the first time, Isis wondered where it came from. Cole seemed so eager, heading into this shift in life eager and seemingly without fear, while every part of it set Isis's teeth on edge. Truthfully, having Cole around with his excitement and confidence did take a bit of the fearful weight off her shoulders – *that* was not something she had anticipated at all.

Before they reached the cashier with their stroller ticket and clothes, Cole paused near an aisle.

"Just a minute."

Leaving Isis with the basket, he stepped down the aisle, spent a few minutes looking at gift-box items at the other end, selected one, and came back.

"What's that?" Isis asked, pointing.

Surprisingly, Cole's cheeks flushed a light pink, and he ran his hands through the curls on his forehead.

He looked abashed and absolutely adorable.

"Well, we are getting all this stuff for the baby, but you're doing all the work. Like, I'll be there cheering you on, but you have to do all the work. And you'll be with the baby more. That's just a sad fact of the world. So I saw these when we first got here and thought you should have something."

His words came out in a rush, and she took the box in her hands as he grabbed the basket from her.

It was a large gift box filled with personal care items – candles, bath oils and gel, aromatherapy lotions, a heating pad, a pretty mug, a silk flower, thick socks – everything she might need to indulge herself. The box read, "For Mom."

"You don't have to get this. I mean, I'm . . ." she blathered.

What? She's fine? Not really. Had plenty of self-care items? Not really. She hadn't bought much indulgent stuff as of late.

That word, *Mom*, caught her in the gut. *I'm going to be a mom!*

"It's not a lot, not compared to everything you are doing, but I want to do something for you."

Words escaped her again. How did he manage to take her by surprise and rob her of logical thought with the most simple of gestures?

Because he didn't *have* to. That was why.

Because he went above and beyond in even the smallest of ways.

She could easily fall in love with him.

Crap.

Who was she kidding? She *was* falling for him. She had been since that night in the hotel room. He seemed easy to fall in love with.

No! It's just your hormones! Get it together, Is!

"Please, take it. Let me do this."

His face, normally bright with a slight smile, looked nervous, as if he was afraid he might be doing the wrong thing. She nodded.

"I love it. Thank you, Cole."

In a quick move she didn't expect, he cupped the back of her head and kissed her forehead.

"No. Thank you."

Chapter Twenty

Cole

After their shopping, Isis offered to stop for lunch, and Cole agreed only if he could pay. She nodded, and they stopped off at a place that cooked specialty ramen noodle bowls.

Their conversation while they slurped noodles amazed him, like their phone calls and texts. Everything with Isis was easy, relaxed, and welcoming. His gaze kept drifting to her sparkling eyes that crinkled when she smiled for real, her lips as she sucked in the long noodles, her slender fingers tipped in dark pink nail polish, her bright hair pulled back in a messy clip.

The more time he spent with her, the more his hard shell cracked. He didn't have to have his iron exterior when she was around – he had nothing to protect himself from. In fact, the need to protect her and the baby grew in inverse proportion.

Hell, being with Isis was like coming home. She found joy in everything.

Including him, it seemed.

From under lowered eyelids, he watched her finish her drink and set her napkin to the side. Her sky-blue shirt, fitted across her full breasts, loosened as it fell to her belly and hips, complementing her hair and making her eyes look more green than gray, and every move she made was with delicate precision.

He was struck at that moment, realizing the significance of this lunch and the shopping and being with Isis and how doing the right thing had to be more than just paying for the baby supplies. It *had* to be.

It meant loving Isis in the way he wanted, in the way she deserved.

He *really* liked this woman and everything about her. His time with her, this beginning together, was much greater, much more significant than previous relationships with girly women who had their eyes full of Marine glory.

Dax called them Barracks Bunnies.

This, here with Isis, *was* something much bigger.

And he knew in his heart he was falling for her hard. He'd felt that spark even before he learned of the pregnancy.

Who was he kidding? He'd felt it since the night in the motel room.

She's even more beautiful because she's glowing, he thought as he surreptitiously watched her.

Maybe it was his emotions or surprising excitement over the baby, or perhaps because he was home from deployment with someone like Isis. Maybe it was the idea that this woman who met him by chance had given him a future, a legacy. Or it was a combination of all three.

The shock of affection and interest in her was real and growing every second.

Just admit it, Corporal! he chastised himself.

He had already fallen for her. He'd lost his heart to her that night nearly a year ago.

The smiling waitress came by to take their trays as he gathered their baby shopping bags, and she noticed the packages.

"Look at you happy parents! You'll have a beautiful baby, I'm sure," she quipped as she made off with their plates. Before she left the table, she leaned over toward Cole. "Your wife is glowing."

He opened his mouth to contradict her about the status of their relationship, but she was gone before the words left his mouth. And why bother? What did it matter if the server thought they were married?

But she spoke a truth that had passed through his mind more than once. He fixed his gaze on Isis, who flipped her eyes to him and quickly lowered them back to her purse.

"Don't even think about it," she stated flatly.

"What? What do you think I was going to say?"

Her hands stopped moving in her purse, and she leveled her eyes at him.

"Oh, please, Cole. I heard what she said to you. I live near a Marine base and hung out with my fair share of military men. I've heard the stories. I know how Marines think."

He knew where her implication was going and bit the inside of his cheek so he didn't burst out laughing. He and Nowak had been cracking jokes of a Marine in another unit who had just become engaged with a woman he'd known all of two weeks. Two weeks!

Now here he was, thinking of marriage to Isis!

"It's an easy answer," she continued, "for a lot of people to say *let's get married because of the baby*, but we barely know each other. This was an unplanned moment, and I don't want you to feel like you have to marry me out of obligation. I don't necessarily want to marry because I have to or out of obligation. I want to marry for love."

Her words struck his chest like a shockwave. She spoke the truth, but his feelings weren't necessarily so black and white. While it would be foolish for them to marry since they had only really connected for the past week, something inside him screamed for more, to try, to see if their magical night, the resulting baby, and this random reconnection, was fate or the universe telling him that they were supposed to be together.

His dick sure as hell thought so. She might be eight months pregnant, but the waitress hadn't lied. Isis was gorgeous.

And his heart wasn't far behind. How many times this week had he thought of her, considered what he could do for her, and reached out with a text or call just to talk to her? How often had he craved a brief word or a quick look at her?

Too often.

Cole just wished he knew where her mind was, and her heart, because her comment about them as a possible couple was not exactly encouraging.

Maybe there was a way to fix that miscommunication.

He reached out and took her cool hand in his. Her touch was like finding a foundation, as though nothing in the world could touch them if they had each other.

"How about this? I was deployed, so we didn't get to know each other well. I didn't get a chance to date you after I met you. Even though we had this no strings attached thing, after our night together, that night meant something. When I was in the desert, I constantly thought about you and wanted to see if I could date you when I returned. It's the whole reason I texted you to begin with. To see if we could finish what we started. So why don't we try to date now? Why don't we see if we do have what it takes to fall in love and get married?"

She didn't pull her hand away, which meant something, but her mouth popped open slightly. "Are you kidding me? That seems like an odd solution to this problem. Especially when I'm hugely pregnant and set to deliver a baby in less than a month."

"Our baby," he corrected. "Remember, this isn't a problem. This is just a quick change of plans, and as I said, I'm really good at adapting. It's what I trained for. Improvise, adapt, overcome."

One blonde eyebrow rose on her clear forehead. "You want to date a pregnant woman? When we have other things to worry about, and I'm as big as a house?"

"You're beautiful, and we seem to be getting those *other things* under control, so there's not much to worry about with the baby. And I like you as big as a house. I'm the one who made you that way, remember?"

He winked and gave her a wry smile. Her mouth popped open again as her cheeks flushed into a flattering shade of rosy-pink, and she looked impossibly more beautiful. Not for the first time, he longed to lean in and kiss her and see where that make-out session went.

After a few breaths, she licked her lips. "Are you serious?"

He shifted closer as if inhaling her breath was the only thing keeping him alive. The heat between them burned hotter than the desert sun.

"I thought I'd made that clear before," he said in a sultry tone. "You're no less beautiful or amazing than you were eight months ago. I'd argue you're more amazing, more beautiful, and I'd be a damned fool to miss out on that. And if dating you also means the possibility of a family, hell, that makes me even more determined."

"Cole," she said with a sigh.

He shifted his face so his lips were close to her ear.

"You had me that night eight months ago. I was yours from that night on. I need you, Isis, and I have to try. For you and for the baby, but also for me."

Isis turned her head slightly, and Cole took advantage of the moment. His lips caught hers in a kiss that was more intense and greedier than he intended. It didn't matter if it was too much. She needed to know how much he craved her. How much he needed her.

And *God!* did he need her!

Her lips responded to his kiss, pressing and urging him on. Cole slid his hand around her hair to cup the back of her head, holding her in place but more afraid to let her go.

He wanted more than one kiss, and if he let go, it might be only one kiss.

And he wanted it all.

His cock was rock hard, and it took every ounce of willpower not to lift her to the table and fuck her here in the restaurant.

Cole moved his lips away and touched his forehead to hers. He exhaled a shaky breath as they lingered together. She took everything from him, and God save him, he wanted her to do it.

"We can start with one date," she said in a breathless voice that made his chest lurch.

Cole didn't stop the side of his lips that curled into his cheek.

He had a foothold in this new, unorthodox relationship, and he'd do everything in his power to keep it.

Isis

It was like all the air was sucked out of Isis's lungs and her mind grew faint.

And she felt like that the entire week. She had to give it to Cole, when he said he wanted to try, he put forth the full effort.

His life became two things – her and the Marines.

The calls and texts increased, and most days, they met up or he came to her parent's place right after training, dropped off by a friend or an Uber. Once he still wore his camo, short-sleeved BDUs, and his hair and face were sweat-damp.

"We went late," he had told her. "But I didn't get to come by yesterday, so I had to come by today."

Conversations between them came so effortlessly, and despite the heaviness of her pregnancy, her mood was buoyant. When they had met up at the small pizza restaurant near the base at the end of the week, he had her laughing to the point of tears.

As much as she hated to admit it, falling for Cole would be far too easy. Her mother had used a phrase once that stuck with

Isis – Cole was easy to love. He wasn't jealous, controlling, or focused on drama, and thus far he had supported every decision she'd made without question.

The level of trust *that* took was shocking.

Then one night at the local coffee bar, she had asked about his family, and that was the first time during week she'd seen his face darken. He recovered quickly, but it was there. She regretted asking – maybe it was too sore a subject?

"My dad died when I was eleven. Heart attack. I have a much older brother, my dad was an older dad when I was born, and my brother Reg is ten years older than me. My mom died my senior year of high school. Stroke." His words held volumes of emotion he dared not speak. He lowered his gaze briefly, then lifted it to look Isis in the eyes. The intensity of his gaze ensnared her as he laid his heart bare. And here she was, living with both her parents at the age of twenty-four! Isis reached her hand over to cover his – a gesture he often did with her when she seemed to struggle, and it never failed to calm her.

"Oh, Cole, I am so sorry to hear that."

He sniffed and ran his other hand through his tight brown curls atop his head. Another familiar gesture that made him look so young and innocent, and it wracked her heart again.

"That's why I joined the Marines. I needed someplace to go, some guidance. The Marines did that for certain. I've been in for eight years now, made it to Corporal, and it just came down this week that I'm up for promotion to Sergeant during the next round of promotions."

The sorrow of his childhood story turned into a shimmery glimmer of hope when he mentioned his promotion. Isis brightened along with him, hoping to deter him away from those hard memories that had darkened his eager face.

"Really? Cole, you must be so excited! I'm so proud!"

For some reason, his cheeks pinkened a bit at her words. Was he embarrassed? Or being modest at her accolade?

Damn, he's cute! was her first, immediate thought before she shoved it from her head. *Get it together, Is!*

Isis couldn't help but smile.

Cole

"What about your parents?" he asked, shifting the topic off himself. "I've met them, but I don't know much about them."

"Typical suburban story. Mom and Dad met in college. She works as a school counselor, and he's a mechanical engineer. I'm an only child."

Cole sat back in his chair with a knowing expression on his face. "That explains a lot about his reaction."

Isis shrugged. "Yep. Overly protective of his only daughter."

Cole's easy expression shifted slightly, and his gaze dropped to her growing abdomen under her shirt – striped this time, and paired with leggings and bare feet clad in thin, black flip flops. He didn't miss how her toes matched her fingernails. He didn't miss anything about her.

"I can understand that completely," he admitted.

"I'm sure you can."

Of course, he could! Not only was he in the same position as her dad – the father of a lone daughter – but he was also a Marine, where protectiveness came second only to patriotism.

"Speaking of my dad, my parents would like you to come over for dinner tomorrow, if you can. Do you have training or anything?"

Dinner with the overbearing father and soon-to-be grandfather. There was nothing Cole wanted to do less.

In truth, he'd rather face a crowd of embassy protesters than her father. He didn't have any emotional ties or want to impress protesters. But if he and Isis were going to make this work, he had to be on board with his daughter's only grandfather.

And he'd do anything to show Isis how much he cared, how much he wanted this to work out between them, how much he lo–

No, he wasn't going there yet. Not in his head, anyway.

Cole cleared his throat and nodded. "If we can make it a bit later, like after six-thirty, I can be showered and changed. I'd rather not show up sweaty and in BDUs again."

She gave him a sly, side-long look as she brushed several locks of her blonde tresses off her shoulder. "Oh, I thought you looked official, all grimy in your BDUs. Very dangerous and Marine-like. It rather turned me on."

The words slid off her tongue with such ease, Cole wasn't sure he heard her correctly at first. Then she innocently took a sip of her drink, as if a comment like that didn't shift the foundation under his feet.

Nope. It was too late. He was already there.

Chapter Twenty-One
Cole

Dinner with the parents went reasonably well, at least in Cole's estimation. Her father, Chaz, didn't glare at him the entire night – only most of it. Cole considered that a win.

Sonia, on the contrary, was overly kind and had tried to make him feel as welcome as possible. She had made a pot roast with vegetables, fresh ones, not the canned crap the mess hall served. Cole couldn't recall the last time he had a real, home-cooked meal. Mess and take-out and MREs lacked a certain flavor and finesse of home-cooked food.

Chaz hadn't spoken much during dinner, and when Sonia announced that she and Chaz were going out for a few hours for movies and drinks with friends, Cole exhaled a low breath.

Maybe the man would simmer down after his granddaughter was born. Otherwise, angry grandpa was going to be a fixture in Cole's life. Yet he was determined to make the best of it. He'd had sergeants and lieutenants who were just as bad, he reminded himself.

He also didn't miss the look that Sonia gave Isis before the front door closed.

"What was that all about?" Cole asked.

Isis rolled her eyes. "Yeah, she wanted us to have some private time. My dad doesn't agree, of course. He thinks we've had enough private time, but my mother pointed out that if we are going to make this work, we need to spend more time together, more than just a meal at a restaurant or a short visit in the backyard."

Considering Cole had been wanting the *exact* same thing, Sonia suddenly moved to the top of his favorite person list.

"Why don't we hang out in the living room, watch a movie, chat, whatever?" she asked.

His mind flashed back to their first night together and how one of his favorite parts of the evening had been just holding her as they talked and dozed.

Damn, he had missed that. That sense of closeness, of oneness. Their connection that night had been solid, complete, and he wanted to touch her, to hold her, and feel that connection again.

The couch in the living room was a plush microfiber mass and when he sat in it, he more sunk in than sat. Isis settled next to him and tried to adjust. With her protruding belly, finding a comfortable spot was proving difficult.

"Here." Cole lifted his arm and tucked her against his chest. He pulled a small pillow away from the arm of the couch and tucked it under her side for leverage. Did it make her more comfortable on the couch? Yes.

Did it also mean she was lying against him? Also yes.

In this one moment with Isis by his side, everything in the world was perfect.

Cole vowed to himself that he had to make this happen with Isis. He *had* to. Not only because she was pregnant, and they were having a daughter together. But because he finally had to admit it. He had fallen madly in love with her – crazy and irrationally in love.

He had fallen for her that first night in that seedy motel. He had been a fool to try and deny that – it just took all this time for him to finally admit it.

But the more important question was, did she love him back? Or was her time and attention on him just to maintain a good relationship for the baby?

Cole exhaled through his nose as Isis flipped the channels. Give him a weapon and an enemy target anytime. As for asking Isis if she felt the same about him, he couldn't bring himself to do it.

Not yet anyway.

So much for the courageous Marine.

They watched mindless television for a bit, and as Isis adjusted her position, his hand fell to her belly.

The gesture seemed so intimate, far too intimate for a casual night of television, but she didn't move his hand. In fact, she covered his long fingers with her hand, holding it in place.

His breath became heavy in his chest.

Any sort of intimacy with her hadn't been discussed or even considered at all. Other than a few steamy kisses that she initiated and drove him mad, he hadn't pushed for anything else. How could he make any request when she was already dealing with so much?

No, he wasn't *that* guy.

Isis adjusted again, and this time her shirt pulled up a bit, and his fingertips rested on bare skin.

It was intimate, raw, and it was almost too much.

"You're killing me, Isis," he said in so low a whisper, he wasn't sure if she even heard him.

He thought she might be shocked or offended. Instead, she sat upright and gave him the most man-eating grin he'd ever encountered in his life. His dick was rock hard under his jeans, and his breaths shuddered with every move of his lungs.

He couldn't resolve his hard-on here – not on her parents' couch. Not without knowing exactly what she wanted from him. And no matter how she smiled at him, she still hadn't said anything about his taking her to bed.

However, his body reacted with a will of its own. The corners of his mouth turned up as he stared at her, and her gray-green gaze met his. With one hand, he brushed her hair off her face, then dropped his thumb to her mouth, tracing her lips.

"What are we doing here, Isis?" he asked gruffly.

"I don't know, Cole. Right now I don't know anything." Her voice was husky as she spoke, reminding him of how her voice sounded all those months ago. His blood pounded through his body, molten lava he couldn't contain.

"You know I want you, Isis, all of you. Every part of you. But right now, I don't feel as if I should do more than what I'm doing."

Her lips tightened against his thumb as she nodded. "I know. I feel that too, like there's too much. Too much baggage. Too much between us. But at the same time. . ."

"Too much for you, but it doesn't have to be that way," Cole commented, and her brow furrowed.

"Cole –" she started to say, but his thumb brushed her full lower lip.

"I don't need anything. You, however, deserve everything. I should be on my knees, before you, ready for anything you might need."

"Cole –" she whispered. Before she could finish the thought, he slid off the couch in front of her. "What are you doing?"

"Everything for you. If you'll let me."

His hands dropped to her hips and he looked up at her with one eyebrow raised. He was asking permission to serve her, and wouldn't move until he received it. No matter how badly his body demanded it. He'd have to take care of himself later. Again.

But it was worth it. She was worth it.

"Cole –" she repeated, and her hand reached out to thread her fingers through the tight curls atop his head. He closed his eyes at her touch. "I've waited so long to do that."

"I've waited, too, Isis. Let me do this for you."

"I don't know if I can do anything more. I'm so huge . . ."

His blood pounded in his head. Looking up at her striking beauty from on his knees between her thighs was like he was worshipping a goddess and exactly where he wanted to be.

"All you have to do is lie back and enjoy. This is all for you."

Her gaze slid down her legs to his face between her legs.

She nodded.

Chapter Twenty-Two

Isis

COLE DIDN'T HESITATE AT all. His fingers curled around her leggings and dragged them off her hips and down her thighs, exposing her full rounded belly and the blonde curls below to him.

She had never felt so exposed, so vulnerable in her life.

How did pregnant women do this? She wondered as his hands danced over her outer thighs, making her skin tingle. She hadn't felt that touch, his touch, in so long. *How did women feel sexy with these bellies? How did men do this when her belly was in the way?*

And most importantly, *why didn't Cole seem to care?*

She knew Cole wanted her. She'd seen and felt his rigid cock press against her more than once over the past couple of weeks. And her own desire skyrocketed whenever any part of him touched her. He lit a lustful flame deep in her belly with every light caress.

That had surprised her. Dealing with pregnancy was tiring, and the last thing she thought she wanted was sexy time. Or so she had believed.

But the moment Cole had stepped through her door again, being with him and anticipating his touch was at the forefront of her mind more than she cared to admit.

What was it about him? About that night? About it all that made her incapable of forgetting him? That made her long for him even more?

It was supposed to be one night, no strings, yet Isis didn't think she would have been able to leave it at that even if she hadn't found out she was pregnant.

Cole's return to the base, then reaching out to her, and committing to her and the baby was beyond her most wild imaginings.

And to now have him on his knees in front of her? Looking at her as though he wanted to consume her whole?

It wasn't possible. But here he was, his curly-cropped brown hair and bright eyes peeking above her thick thighs and round belly.

His hand curled around her hips where they met the upper curve of her plentiful ass cheeks and pressed lightly.

"Slide down for me."

For me.

His voice was little more than a husky breath in the incandescent glow, like a feather, enticing and commanding her at the same time.

She couldn't deny him.

Who was she kidding? Since that fateful night nearly nine months ago, she knew she'd deny him nothing.

His fingertips dug lightly into her skin again, and she slid down until she was at the edge of couch, giving him full access to the space between her thighs. His hands slipped over the tops of her legs to her inner thigh, and pressed lightly again.

"Open for me, Isis."

His words rolled off his tongue and made her shiver.

"You can't," she protested weakly. "You'll suffocate."

The corner of his eyes crinkled as he gazed up at her. "Then I'll die a happy man. Open for me."

She shifted so her legs parted.

Her view of her upper thighs might be obscured, but parting her legs gave him full view. And full access.

With delicate precision, his lips first touched her inner thigh, molten-hot, and the intimacy of his touch after so long removed, made her insides melt. His hands moved to grip the soft skin of her thighs before his lips caressed upward, trailing hot kisses up her legs to the nest of dark blonde curls at the apex of her thighs.

His face nuzzled those curls, and her head fell back on the couch as she gasped.

The sensation was mind-blowing. It had been so long since his touch that his kisses, his tongue, and even the light press of his face between her thighs brought a thrum of pleasure surging through her.

Then his tongue moved, parting her slit, and her hands grabbed the cushions beside her.

The effect of his touch was immediate and jolting.

If she could have reached his head to grab it, she would have. Instead, she had to clench her fingers into the couch as every nerve ending vibrated through her.

Then the tip of his tongue brushed over her clit.

Her keening gasp echoed in the room as her insides surged, that thrum of pleasure swelling as the world fell away and there was only herself and his tongue.

Over and over with slow precision, Cole's tongue stroked her pulsing button until she was writhing on the couch, begging him for something, anything. She didn't know what because her mind had left and was on another plane.

How long had she craved this? Longed for his touch? Longed for the man himself?

Then his licking changed. His lips thrust deeper, and he sucked lightly on her clit.

She arched off the couch as much as her body would let her and screeched Cole's name as thrumming liquid heat exploded inside her, turning her entire body to purring liquid as uncontrollable ecstasy flooded her. Her orgasm was made more powerful because of how long she had waited for this.

For him.

As she crested back to earth and her body sagged into the couch, Cole sat back and his flashing, arctic blue eyes skimmed over her spent form. The side of his glistening lip turned up in his familiar, sensuous and satisfied smile.

Then, with the same delicateness as when he worshiped her thighs and clit with his lips, he tugged at her leggings and she shifted so he could pull them up and over her legs and hips again.

So proper, and she giggled shakily at his sense of propriety. He joined her on the couch, sitting close, and placed his arm around her back.

The gesture was so comfortable, so easy, especially since he had just feasted on her. He made all of this confusing mess seem simple. How did he do that when her mind raced and she was exhausted merely thinking about it? The way he put her at ease and made her feel adored increased her interest and desire for him, and she wondered if there was anything he *couldn't* do.

His bright gaze never left her face. She reached out her hand and traced the chiseled lines of his jaw to the dimple in his chin.

"What was that about, Cole?" she whispered, breaking the heady silence.

His glittering eyes narrowed. "What do you mean?"

Yes, what did she mean? She could barely think, let alone question his motives.

"Why did you want to do that?"

Cole stiffened, and his dancing eyes hardened. "Why are you asking me that? Because I wanted to go down on you? Because

I've missed being with you? Because I wanted to watch you come because I love that? Because *I* needed it?"

Isis turned slightly to face him. The position twinged her belly, and she frowned slightly.

"This all seems so crazy. We haven't seen each other in eight months. I barely know you, and here we're having a baby. I'm huge and feel so unsexy and find it impossible that you would want to think of me that way at all. Why would you do that? What are we doing here?"

Thank god she had just orgasmed, or her own questions would have brought tears to her eyes. Though his face appeared hard, his lips softened, full and pouting.

"I thought I was showing you that when I said I was committing, I meant it. If I go down on you to make you happy, then it makes *me* happy. Hell, Isis, I've never met anyone like you, and I've been all over the fucking world. We thought that night was an end, but it was really a start, a start for us, and I'm willing to follow that road all the way. Over the past few weeks, I –"

He stopped abruptly, as did her heart in her chest.

"What?"

"I can't lie. I'm falling for you, hard. No, I've fallen for you. I started falling for you that night last year, and every moment I'm with you, I just want you more. I know you think we should shut it down, that we don't know each other. But I know I want to be with you, I *need* to be with you. Call me a fool, but I'm in love with you, and I do want to marry you. Not for benefits or for the baby or because it's the right thing to do. I want to marry you for *you*."

Before she could answer or even catch her breath, he bent to her and claimed her lips in a deep, sensual kiss, a kiss that spoke louder than his words, as if he was pouring all his love, all his emotion, all his need into that one kiss.

And Isis kissed him back, meeting the fervor of his lips.

Her mind was muddled, though, a mess of her thoughts and her own emotions. Mainly because, though she tried to deny it, she felt so much the same.

That Cole might want to be with her for her wasn't something she readily accepted, but here she was in this situation with this astounding, handsome man who had feelings for her and said he wanted to marry her, to spend the rest of his life with her.

What was she supposed to do with that? Could she marry a man she had known for both nine months yet only a few weeks? A man she had no reason to fall in love with, but had done so anyways? The paradox was the last thing she considered before his hand slid around her jaw to cup the back of her head, drawing her even closer.

Like he was claiming her for his own with this one kiss.

Cole

He'd said too much, Cole knew. He kept his hard outer shell with his men, but with Isis, she cracked that shell and shoved it aside until there were only his sappy emotions. And in truth, he didn't feel like he needed a shell when he was with her. As if he could show her the most vulnerable parts of himself and nothing would harm him.

Those emotions he didn't deal with well – emotions that he poured onto her all at once. No wonder she didn't respond directly when he mentioned marriage.

Again.

Yet, what did he expect her to say as he practically declared his love for her and asked her to marry him? That she'd throw herself at him? She was on the verge of giving birth. His declarations of love and marriage were probably the last thing on her mind.

Isis, however, didn't pull away, and Cole saw that as a positive thing. She kissed him hard when he had to leave, and departing her side that night was one of the most difficult things he'd ever done.

The last time he'd left her after a passionate night, he hadn't seen her for eight months.

And he had created a daughter with her.

Cole admitted to himself he never wanted to leave her side again. The barracks had become his prison, separating them, but to get base housing with Isis, they needed to be married.

After how she reacted to the question the night before, Cole came to the conclusion it would be better if he took a break in asking. She wasn't ready, even if his heart was there. He didn't want to pressure her too much, especially right now when she was set to deliver in a couple of weeks.

He'd just have to *show* her that he was serious about her and their relationship.

When Cole returned to base, Marines still milled about the barracks, ready for lighter duty during the weekend. Several privates played cards at the game tables in the community room near the entry. Cole nodded to the Marines who called out hello before taking the stairs two at a time to the second floor barracks.

Lance Corporal David Sorell was at his trunk, putting away several stacks of clothes. He glanced at Cole before returning his attention to his packing.

"Have you heard the rumor?" he asked Cole.

Cole froze. In the Marines, rarely did good news crest on a wave of rumors. He crossed over to his bed and opened his own trunk to lock up his wallet and get out a t-shirt and shorts for sleeping.

"Nope. What have you heard?"

David slammed the trunk lid and locked it, then turned his high-and-tight blonde head to Cole. He wore his reading glasses. The guy had lucked out, being far-sighted in the military. He might not be able to read fine print, but Sorell could snipe a hawk diving into the grass from almost five clicks away without a scope. It was uncanny.

"You might not like it," Sorell answered. "When's your girl due?"

Cole's face stiffened as he adopted his stern visage while his chest hollowed.

"Like two weeks? Three? It's a first baby, so . . ."

He let the words linger, waiting for David to let him in on the rumor. David tilted his head thoughtfully.

"Then you'll be okay. Warrant Officer Berette hinted that we might be heading back to Saudi in late July."

Late July? Shit, that was less than four months!

His teeth clenched. Cole had hoped to get everything together with Isis before he left so she and the baby were fully cared for.

There was no way they'd be married in four months.

He had expected a six-month Stateside station at Pendleton. Maybe more if they got lucky. That was what had happened last time.

Fuck. Less than four months.

"So what are you gonna do, Maxton?"

Cole's jaw was rigid, hiding the roiling emotions that threatened to burst out of his chest. He put on his iron shell and tucked his folded shirt under his arm.

"I guess I'm going to have a baby."

It wasn't an answer – his entire squad already knew that, but what else could he say?

Fuck. Four months.

"You thinking of marrying her?"

Cole's jaw clenched again, but he didn't answer.

David flopped back on his cot and lifted his glasses to his forehead. "Oh, shit. Don't tell me you asked her already!"

"A lot of guys get married to women after knowing them for only a few months. Especially if she gets pregnant. That's nothing new."

David slapped the bed. "Hell, Maxton! They at least know her for a few months! You've only been with Isis for like three weeks!"

"Nine months. Don't forget we met before I deployed."

"Fuck no. You *hooked up* before you deployed. So three weeks and a day. I don't know a single Marine who tied the knot *that* fast."

A muscle in Cole's jaw twitched, and David must have seen it. He stopped laughing and sat up.

"Brother, really. I think it's crazy to think about marrying her this soon. Just be a co-parent baby daddy and call a day. You can get married later. Speaking of which, let me know if you need anything. My sister just had a baby with her Army husband, so I have a contact at least if you need information or advice."

Cole dipped his head slightly to acknowledge the offer. It was far too kind, even if the ass-hat lance corporal did think he was crazy for considering marriage.

"Hell, Sorell. Army? Your sister a traitor or just slumming?"

David chuckled and grabbed his own white tee from his bed.

"There's no accounting for taste. And she married him before I entered the Corps, so I can't blame her too much."

Chapter Twenty-Three
Cole

Cole had done as he promised himself and hadn't mentioned his inopportune love for Isis or marriage again.

The good thing was, it seemed she didn't hold his passionate ardor against him, having met him several more times, set up another visit with her parents, and went on a final shopping trip over the weekend.

However, something had changed with Isis, and Cole had noticed it as they walked the local mall. Isis was slower, waddling hard, and seemed a bit breathless. More than once, she put her hand under her belly, making Cole spring into protector mode.

"Is everything okay?" he had asked as he rushed to hold her back.

Isis had given him a thin smile and nodded. "Yeah. Just so tired. I'm set to deliver in a week, so my body's just getting ready. And I'm so freaking tired of being pregnant and huge."

She had been breathless as she spoke. Cole didn't know much about babies, but it seemed like the baby might not wait a week. He had escorted her toward a collection of couches near a smoothie bar and helped her sit. Isis exhaled hard once settled.

"Do you want something to eat or drink? Water or a smoothie?"

Her pale face had brightened as she looked up at him.

"A strawberry smoothie would be great."

Cole bolted upright. "I'm on it."

He had rushed toward the counter, and Isis leaned forward as far as she could on the couch. "With a vitamin boost please!"

Cole had lifted his hand to acknowledge her request and returned shortly with a tall, pink smoothie for her and a bottle of water. Having a just-in-case bottle of water was always good practice, whether it was to combat desert heat or for a thirsty pregnant woman.

Later that afternoon, she dropped him off at the barracks, she was pale again, and Cole had asked her to text him when she got home to make sure she was okay. He had the realization that he was going to need to get a car. Though he hadn't seen the need for one while deployed, unlike some Marines on base, now that he was going to be a dad, getting a car moved much higher on his list of needs. He couldn't have Isis driving him around like this any longer, especially once the baby came.

Privates Sheedy and Cortes were car-heads. Maybe they could guide him in the right direction, and he made a mental note to ask about where to get a car and fast.

The following week was the start combat training, which pleased Cole. He was looking to promote to Sergeant within the next two years, and his combat training score made up a large portion of points towards promoting. Working as a combat instructor for the day added to that score, and every set of new recruits meant a lot of focused training, so they didn't blow off their own appendages or someone else's.

Monday morning before 6 am was cool and cloudy, the perfect weather for training. Nothing worse than scorching heat or drenching rain. Cool and cloudy meant a better day, no matter what happened.

Combat training mostly focused on the new recruits, and Marines who were updating their training lined up behind the recruits in the training field for live fire training. Littered with faux, torn-up concrete buildings, concrete blocks, and random decommissioned tanks and trucks, it was a dangerous place. Anything regarding explosives was dangerous.

Lt. Jackson was the officer on deck that morning, with Staff Sgt. Drake as the other combat training instructor. The recruits' drill instructor, a fine sergeant named Watanabe, and his stern glare never left his recruits.

The day began with a series of safety training, which was like talking to a wall for some of these recruits. That was the most tricky part of the day – making sure the recruits fully understood the dangers of M-67 fragmentation grenades and used them correctly.

One mistake and someone was going home without a leg, or worse.

But these dumb newbs never paid enough attention, and more than once in the past, Cole had to grab a private and throw him out of the way of an improperly handled or thrown grenade.

Cole and Drake flanked Jackson as he strode back and forth in front of the line, explaining the details of the day. Cole's camo BDU cap was pulled low on his forehead to cut any dull sun glare and hid his close-cropped curls. Only the edged-up shaved part of his hair was exposed per Marine combat dress standards, and the low brim made him look more authoritative.

When Lt. Jackson was finished with his lecture, Cole and Drake split up the recruits and those up for review training and began the intensive safety protocol. Once the recruits passed that rigorous round of lecture and hands-on practice, they could move to live fire grenades.

About a dozen Marines followed Cole to a clear section of the field that held several pieces of gear and the two types of grenade training, offensive and defensive.

As Cole explained the safety protocol for grenade handling and showed them the difference between the two grenades usages, he noted more than one recruit drifting off.

Fuck.

That meant problems. Significant problems.

"Recruit! Is this too boring for you?"

At his shout of the word recruit, Watanabe was immediately at Cole's side, adding his own shouting lecture to the recruit.

"Recruit! Do you have something better to do than listen to your Corporal? Do you have someplace more important than this where you will learn to not only save your life but the lives of your fellow Marines?"

Cole's lips tightened at Watanabe's words. Being a Drill Sergeant was one of the hardest jobs in the Corps, and Cole was glad it was Watanabe in that position. The guy had his drill instructor shit down and his recruits were usually some of the best trained when they promoted to Private.

How sad for Watanabe to have gotten a bad apple this time around.

"No, Drill Sergeant!" the recruit shouted. At least he held his own with his tone and demeanor when called out for his lazy behavior.

"Then pay attention! Corporal Maxton's instruction will one day save your life."

"Yes, Drill Sergeant!"

Watanabe nodded to Cole who resumed his lecture.

No one else drifted off for the rest of the morning.

Cole

By midday, the recruits had grenades in hand. The goal was to practice with fakes, then they moved to the debris field and threw live grenades from behind the protective wall.

Cole held a fake grenade over his head. "Pull the pin, and as you throw it, shout *frag out!* This tells all your other Marines that a live grenade is in play. If you do not do this, you risk your life and the lives of your fellow Marines. Do you understand?"

"Yes, Corporal!" they shouted in unison.

Then they moved to live rounds. They took turns, throwing their grenades and exploding the ground on the far side of the wall.

The new recruit from earlier, the one who Watanabe had called out, was up next. Cole kept a sharp eye on him since the kid had been asleep for part of the training.

"Do you know what to do, recruit? Pull, throw and shout, and duck."

"Yes, Corporal," he answered in a confident tone.

Surprisingly, the recruit did just as instructed and threw his grenade perfectly. It caused an eruption of dirt and debris in the field about 15 yards away.

Nice arm.

Cole paused to let the dirt settle and make sure the field was clear before the next recruit stepped up. He raised his hand to halt the practice when he saw a young recruit exposed to the live fire field, clearing away debris from the other protective wall next to them.

And at that same one, another recruit from his group had moved to the platform and took his grenade.

All Cole heard was "Frag out!" and Cole was running in an instant.

He raced around the edge of the protective wall to where the young recruit stood as he brushed away debris and dragged him behind the protective shield as the grenade exploded. They made it right as the ground shot up with dirt and debris. A few small particles of ground and grass dust rained down against Cole's backside as he and the young recruit fell into the protected side of the partition.

"Are you okay?" Cole asked the kid as he brushed dirt off his hat and the recruit's.

This was not the day he was supposed to have, nearly getting blown to bit. *Fuck!* If he had been any slower, this could have ended badly, both for the recruit and himself.

The stricken kid nodded, and Cole slapped him on the back and released him to Sgt. Drake's care.

Drill Sergeant Wantanbe was already on the grenade-throwing recruit's case, screaming at him for his inattention that could have gotten both Cole and the new recruit killed.

"Do you want to be recycled? Lt. Jackson is right there! Come on, you're going with him to the Command Office."

Then the kid was gone, being dragged away by Jackson, whose face was a mask of absolute fury.

Fuck ups like that were not acceptable in the Marine Corps. In addition to recycling and being pushed back in training for a few weeks, that recruit was going to have to do pushups and run until he puked. Several times.

Cole had no pity for the kid. Marines had to learn that this wasn't a game, that these were real weapons. Lives were at stake with everything they did, and their training was what made them the best military unit in the world. It saved lives, both their own and other's.

And this kid nearly took all that, and his future with his baby and Isis, away from him. It was too close a call. Way too close.

Fuck.

Cole spat on the ground and tried to quell his surging anger that simmered inside him. One stupid mistake could have cost him everything. Could have cost Isis and baby Aurore everything.

Fuck.

No, he wasn't going to let that happen. He wasn't going to risk getting killed, or getting deployed and not coming back until Isis knew how he felt, and he knew how she felt about him. No more dancing around it.

He loved her, he was going to tell her, and he was going to tell his daughter every single day that he loved her. And God help him, he'd convince Isis to marry him on top of it all.

Life was too short to live with any regrets.

And he was not going to regret anything with Isis.

Chapter Twenty-Four
Cole

On the training field, he kept his phone and wallet in a lockbox in the command trailer. It was near the end of the day when he yanked his BDU hat off his head and wiped the grime off his face with it. He was covered in a film of dirt and dust.

Sgt, Drake followed him into the trailer, griping about the lowly nature of these new recruits, and went to his lockbox.

He was the only one in the trailer when Cole clicked on his phone.

A text message from Isis.

No. Not a text message. Several messages.

And a few missed phone calls.

Oh no.

He clicked the text message icon and a series of messages from Isis scrolled across his screen.

She was in the hospital.

Delivering their daughter.

"Fuck!" he shouted as he frantically looked at the time when the message was sent. *Noon? How long did it take to deliver a baby?* "Fuck!"

Sgt. Drake leaned back to study him with a curious gaze. "Everything okay, Iron Maxton?"

Cole stared at his phone and shook his head. "No. Isis is in labor. Shit, she's been in labor for five hours." His head swiveled to Drake. "How long does it take to have a baby? Do you know?" He was already selecting her phone number to call. It went straight to voicemail.

Shit.

Drake tilted his head as if he was listening for the universe to answer. "No. It's always fast in the movies, but I heard that's all fake."

Cole shoved his phone and wallet into his BDU cargo pocket. "I gotta get a ride. I need to get to the hospital now. I need –"

Drake pushed himself off the trailer wall, jingling his keys. "I got you, brother. Come on. You tell the lieutenant you gotta go for a family emergency, and I'll bring my truck around."

He slapped Cole's upper arm and strode out of the trailer, then broke into a run once he hit the ground.

Cole joined him outside and ran with long strides to Lt. Jackson and saluted fast.

"Lieutenant, I have a family emergency!"

Jackson rolled one broad shoulder to the side as he half turned to Cole. "Your lady? Is she having the baby?"

Fuck, rumors were more contagious than the fuckin' flu!

"Yes, Lieutenant. I gotta to go."

Jackson waved his hand toward the field. "Then go. Let us know the good news once you have it."

Cole saluted again and broke into a full run toward Drake's silver pickup that was bouncing onto the grass through the front of the field. He jumped into the cab as soon Drake slowed enough for Cole to reach the door.

Sgt. Drake didn't wait for the door to close before he peeled out, kicking up dirt back to the road. Then they were on the pavement, speeding toward the main gate.

Cole grabbed his phone and kept calling.

What a shit day this had been. He'd nearly had his nuts blown off by a stupid, overeager recruit and now he might be missing the birth of his baby.

He puffed out a frustrated breath but didn't let those thoughts go any further.

The last thing he wanted to do was curse himself and wonder what else could go wrong.

Cole

Cole was out of the car before Drake brought it to a stop and slammed the truck door closed as his boots thundered to the entrance.

He stood out horribly, tall and filthy in his BDUs, but he didn't care who stared. There was only one thing that held his focus – Isis. And the baby.

A kindly woman in scrubs behind the desk looked him up and down.

"Can I help you, hon?"

Her tone was polite and for that, Cole was grateful.

"Yes, ma'am. My girlfriend is here. Having a baby."

The woman turned to the computer and typed. "What's her name?"

"Oh, Jennings. Isis Jennings."

Her eyes slanted toward him. "And you are . . .?"

"Uh, the father?"

Hearing the words aloud made his mind reel.

She licked her smiling lips. "I presumed that already. Your name, dear. I need to print you a wristband."

"Oh. Cole. Corporal Cole Maxton."

Her fingers danced across the keyboard. "Got it."

She took the plasticky band from the printer and grabbed his arm. With a skillful move of her fingers, she had it on his wrist in the blink of an eye.

"Alright, Dad. Go through those double doors and take the elevator up to three. The maternity security door is right when you step out. They will check your band and take you to mom."

Shit. Dad and *mom* were names and identities he hadn't thought about yet. Hearing someone call them by those names made it difficult to focus on her words.

As soon as she finished her instructions, he took off in a run for the elevators. He was at the security doors and in the maternity ward within seconds.

He wasn't wasting any time. He was late enough as it was.

"Isis is in delivery right now," the short nurse at the door told him as she led him inside.

"Can I –?" Cole glanced down at his filthy BDUs. There was no way he could be with her when he was this dirty.

"She's starting to push, but that could take some time yet." She turned to her desk and gave him a clear bag with blue clothing in it. Scrubs.

"Use the bathroom there, wash off as much as you can, and change into these. Put your clothes in the bag, and I'll put them in her room."

Cole nodded and shot into the bathroom, scrambling to wash and change at the same time. Once he thought he was clean enough, he shoved his clothes into the bag and joined the nurse. It wasn't ideal, but the scrubs were a far sight cleaner than his field BDUs.

"Okay, let me take you to the door but wait until I bring you in. I need to clear it with Mom and see if anyone is in the room who might need to leave."

While he hoped there was enough room for both him and Sonia, he had the sinking sensation that if there wasn't, Isis would want her mother there. He wouldn't blame her in the least.

Isis knew and trusted Sonia a hell of a lot more than she knew him, father of the baby or not.

He wondered for a moment where Chaz was.

Probably looking for a shotgun, Cole thought sourly.

The short nurse returned and smiled at him. "Okay, Dad. The doctor says there's enough room, and Isis says she wants you here, so come on in."

His stomach clenched into a Gordian knot as he stepped through the doorway and into the unknown.

It was nearly as bad as a battlefield, and after this, no one would ever be able to convince him that women didn't fight just as vigorously, if not more, in this battle than any Marine.

The doctor, a thin woman in a white coat, crouched at Isis's feet, her powerful voice as strong as a five star general commanding troops. She was calling for Isis to push while the assisting nurse raced between Isis and the doctor. It was louder and more chaotic than he had ever imagined.

Sonia was at Isis's left side, holding her hand and speaking low and encouragingly. Cole couldn't make out a single word, but the tone buzzed to calm her.

"Over there, Dad," the labor and delivery nurse pointed to the right side of the bed near Isis's head. Cole moved up next to her, a grim, frozen smile on his lips.

Her bright blonde hair was half pulled up in a scrunchie while loose strands were plastered against the side of her sweaty, pale face. Her light freckles stood out sharply, and her green eyes dulled from exhaustion and probably pain.

With no idea of what he was supposed to do, he clasped her hand and kissed her damp forehead.

"Cole . . ." she breathed out.

He gazed at her face with the most encouraging look he could muster.

"I just got your message and raced here. I'm here. Your mom is here. We're all supporting you."

A broken smile tugged at her chapped lips, but before she could say or do anything else, the doctor spoke up.

"Okay, Isis. We're trying again. This time really push, and if you push hard enough, she just might come out. She's ready to meet you."

In a shockingly quick move, Isis leaned impossibly forward with Sonia pressing on her back. Cole did the same, helping her hold forward. Then for a long count of ten, Isis clenched her eyes shut, and the loudest, longest screeching scream emanated from deep inside her, something primal and raw and forceful.

The sound and power behind it vibrated to Cole's core as the doctor counted and Sonia and the nurse shouted encouraging words.

Cole didn't know what to do, so he held her hand and her back and pressed his head close to hers.

This birthing thing was nothing like what they showed on television. No matter how much the Marine Corps prepared him for every aspect of war and battle, nothing he had ever learned or trained for could have prepared him for this.

Then a squalling that pierced the air.

His daughter!

"It's a girl!" the doctor shouted over the squall, and Isis flopped back into the bed, the tightness in her face gone in a wash of relief.

They brought the baby to Isis. Cole stared in complete shock as Isis cuddled and cooed at this new life they had created together.

Isis tore her gaze from Aurore to him, her eyes so full of love, his heart stopped pounding in his chest.

Is the earth tilting? It's tilting...

"She's beautiful," Isis said breathlessly.

Everything happened so fast from that moment. The nurse took the baby back, then tugged on his arm, bringing him to a small plastic bed under a bright light where the pink howling baby lay.

His baby.

His Aurore.

His insides were gone, melted, hollowed out in a mix of pure joy and the most dire fear.

He was a dad now, and this screaming little girl was going to rely on him for everything.

How could he do that? What if he didn't measure up? What did he know about being a dad?

The Corps hadn't prepared him for this at all!

He started to look over his shoulder at Isis to see if she was okay, but the nurse returned and was scrubbing the baby. Hard. What was she doing?

"Here, Dad, We're going to get all that blood pumping and make sure she's breathing and has good color."

After the baby was howling over the aggressive rub-down, the nurse took a damp cloth and wiped off all the birthing remnants, which contributed to her pinkiness. Wiped clean, Aurore was less bright pink, and her scream had turned to shuddering cries.

As he stood stupefied, watching the scene around him, the nurse expertly handled the baby, put her in a diaper and the tiniest shirt imaginable, and finally wrapped her in a white and blue hospital baby blanket.

Once the baby was bundled, the nurse handed the quieted, burrito-styled baby to him and his awkward, incompetent arms.

"It's okay, Dad. Just hold her like this. Let's take her over to mom."

Cole gingerly held his daughter so Isis could see the baby while the doctor and nurse did their jobs.

"I'm glad you made it in time." Isis's voice was little more than a weary rasp.

Cole swallowed and nodded. His eyes didn't leave the tiny, round face peeking out from the blanket. Her hair was light, little more than pale peach fuzz, and she had the tiniest cleft in her rounded chin.

His heart shattered.

His cleft chin.

"She is the most amazing thing I've ever seen."

Isis moved her hand and rested it on his arm, and he finally turned his gaze from the baby to Isis, and even completely worn and battered, she was stunningly beautiful. His heart wrenched impossibly more.

He stared at her, committing this moment of her beauty and the delicate weight of the baby in his arm to memory.

This moment with his new family was one he wanted to remember for the rest of his life.

Chapter Twenty-Five
Cole

THE NEXT DAY WAS mostly a blur. Isis dozed on and off, but the nurses scurried in and out of the room throughout the night, so no one really got any sleep. Except maybe Aurore.

All the baby did was eat, sleep, and poop, and the nurses had to show him how to change a diaper, which was far more complicated than he had realized. How did her legs keep getting caught in the waist? Why didn't her legs straighten at all?

The gentle tinkling of Isis's laughter as he mangled the first two diaper changes was music to his ears.

As both mom and baby were recovering well, they were hoping to discharge her the following morning – though Cole couldn't imagine her going home only one day after everything Isis just experienced. Sonia had left to get the house ready for their arrival. But as Cole was the father, the nurses set up a small chair bed thing in the corner of the recovery room for him to sleep on.

By the end of the day, the hectic nature of everything had calmed. Isis was dozing, and when Aurore stirred, he rose from his corner chair and lifted her out of the plastic bassinet.

He wore a second pair of scrubs because the nurses didn't want anything to do with his filthy BDUs, but the scrubs were comfortable, and he didn't mind looking like a hospital employee. It was merely another uniform.

Lifting Aurore out of her bassinet, he cuddled her close to his chest and made shushing noises to soothe her. The tiny baby curled toward his chest and once she was in the position she wanted, Aurore's delicate eyelids closed.

Everything about the baby was so perfect, from her nearly translucent skin to the gentle curve of her cheek to her tiny, pursed lips. Cole sat in his weird chair and settled in with the baby.

He knew it was probably a feeling all new dads had, but he felt like he could look at her forever.

So many emotions roiled inside him, a tumultuous storm of every emotion possible. How was he supposed to be a dad when his had died before he was a man? And to be a dad to a daughter? What did he know about little girls? Then to have this tiny being rely on him for everything? How could he do that when he was deploying in a few months?

She would be an entirely different person when he returned to the States, and he had to blink back fiery tears at how this one dainty, swaddled person now meant everything in the world was different.

A shifting sound came from the bed, and his jaw tightened as he looked up at Isis. Her gray eyes were both loving and intense as her gaze rested on him and Aurore, and he didn't want her to see him cry.

And he was failing at it.

"Hey, babe. You okay?" Isis asked.

A thick breath jerked out of his chest, and the baby squirmed before settling again.

"Am I okay?" he replied in a hushed voice. "I didn't do anything but show up late. You did all the work. Are you okay?"

She grimaced a bit as she adjusted into more of a sitting position, then a calm expression crossed her face.

"Sore, yeah. And bone tired. That was so much work. And my throat hurts."

A hint of a smile tipped the corners of his mouth. "Probably from the screaming. I didn't know you could make those sounds."

Her own smile played across her lips. "Yeah. I can be loud when I need to."

"I think you needed to," he said as he looked down at the baby, then back at Isis. "It seems like it was worth it."

Her smile faltered.

"Do you think it was worth it? This is going to be a lot of work. Do you regret this at all?"

Such a harsh question and he hated that she felt the need to ask it. Yet he also understood. Cole had to swallow the hard lump that formed in his throat. How could he begin to tell her what this meant to him, what the baby and she meant to him?

He didn't have the words.

He tried to use his eyes, to let his gaze pour onto her all the love and joy and fear that spun like a tempest inside him.

"This changes everything," he finally said in a shaky, awe-filled tone. "I don't know what to do with her. How to be a dad to her. I'm just stricken right now."

Isis gave him a tired smile and dipped her chin.

"Improvise, overcome, adapt. Isn't that what you said? Well, we improvised hard, overcame, and now we'll adapt. Look at all you've done for her before she was even here. You're adapting just fine, and you'll do even better with practice."

He blinked hard, his chest heaving. How was she comforting him after all she'd just been through? Add it to the reasons he loved her. Though he hadn't told her yet, that list was growing longer by the day.

"Cole, are you okay? Are you crying? Is something wrong?" Concern for his well being filled her voice.

"I'll need the practice," he told her. "I don't have family. And I never really did. My older brother was out of the house before I was a teenager and I haven't spoken to him much since. My parents died when I was still a kid. I don't have anyone, any family. I only had the Corps. But now I have her, and you, and I have a family."

His lips quivered as he spoke and he flicked his gaze from Isis to the baby, and back to Isis.

"That's a gift I never imagined I'd have. In dreams maybe, but not in reality. You gave that to me, Isis. You gave me a gift I never dreamed possible. It's like the world was just dull shades of color, but you and her, you have brought vibrant color into my world. I see the world differently now. I cannot thank you enough. And this gift, her, this family, only makes me love you more."

Her eyes flashed as he said it. He was laying it all on the line, and he no longer cared who knew how he felt. He had vowed to himself that he'd have no regrets and he was going to live by that vow.

"Cole, please . . ." she whispered.

"I know now's not the time," he continued, "but I have to say it. I know firsthand, between my parents and being a Marine, life is so precarious, so fragile, and we squander it. But if I'm a fool for saying it, for feeling how I feel, then I'd rather be a fool who took the chance at life. Because this could all be gone tomorrow, and I'm not going to be one who squandered it. I love her. I love you. I want to marry you, and I want you to know that."

Chapter Twenty-Six

Isis

THIS TIME, ISIS HAD to blink back weary, emotional tears.

Seeing Cole sitting in that extended chair, his long, muscled frame curved over the bundled baby as if he'd never held anything so fragile in his life, made her entire body throb with emotion. His handsome face, which could look so tough when necessary, was tense and stricken, as if he still couldn't believe the evidence of their one night he held in his arms.

Hell, neither could she. The past year had been a whirlwind of emotions and surprises, and it had all led to this one quiet moment in her hospital room with Cole and Aurore.

Cole . . . what was she going to do about him?

Though they had spent nearly all of their free time together over the past few weeks, she really only knew him a few weeks.

Was that enough to fall in love? To build a life? To get married?

Her soft gaze landed on the strong Marine turned to mush with the arrival of their baby girl.

Though her rational mind tried over and over to convince her otherwise, she *did* love him.

Cole was easy to love. Isis knew it because her heart and mind had fallen into agreement over her feelings for him. It could be hormones or the security he offered, but those eyes...

In the end, it came back to the brilliant blue eyes that were chips of ice when he was angry or pools of azure seas when he looked at her.

And when he looked at her...

It was like everything in the world stopped and there was only Cole and herself.

She shouldn't feel that way – the logical part of her brain endeavored to tell her that daily – but her heart had won that battle.

And watching him with their new daughter only strengthened her heart.

He said he loved her and wanted to marry her. But everything seemed so rushed. He claimed to have asked her because of how he felt about her, but how much of that was truth and how much was a result of the child he now held and his overdeveloped sense of obligation?

Then again, wasn't that love, too? Once there was a connection, wasn't it followed by sense of obligation toward that person, a desire to support them in life, to help them become the best person they can be?

Cole had returned his gaze to the baby, and now lifted his face to look at her in a look that shared all the love his lips proclaimed. She was a mess, tired, and felt crusty, but he gazed at her as though she was everything for him, a gaze full of unconditional love and adoration. And her heart wrenched in her chest.

Was there any one way to define what love was? Poets and philosophers had tried, writing dense tomes of the nature of love, yet each one missed the mark in some way. There was no way to define love, as it shifted and changed over time and from person to person.

Who was to say that what she and Cole had built over the past year wasn't love, as unorthodox as it was?

Because the longer they shared that gaze and drank in each other, the more she realized that love was what she made it, what *they* made it together.

Love was Aurore, and Cole, and her relationship with him.

And if her heart wanted to love him, then she would.

Shifting awkwardly in her bed again, she gestured to the bassinet beside her.

Silently, Cole brought the sleeping baby to the bassinet, and with delicate movements, his muscled arms placed Aurore in the baby bed. He then turned to Isis, his blue gaze cutting through the dim light of the nighttime hospital room.

He looked absolutely adorable in the gifted scrubs. Isis patted the narrow strip of mattress next to her.

His face looked hurt. "I don't know if I should. What if I hurt you?" He pointed to the chair in the corner. "That flips out into a bed-like cot thing."

Her lips pulled into a soft smile, and she moved the thin blanket and patted the bed again.

"You won't hurt me," she said in a husky whisper.

Cole blinked once then moved with the ease of someone used to quick action. He went to the other side of the bed and gently climbed in, pressing lightly against her slightly turned backside, curling his long form protectively around her.

The sensation brought back a rush of memories of the last time they had lain like this, in the cheap hotel room nine months before, in that frozen-frame moment of perfection.

His arm slid to her shoulder, pausing in its tender touch. "Is this okay?" His breath blew against her loose hair on her ear, tickling. "I don't know what's okay."

Isis reached up and grasped his hand, moving it to her side as she threaded her fingers with his. The strength and weight of his hand on her grounded her, telling her more than anything that all was right in the world, and she was exactly where she was supposed to be.

"Everything you are doing is okay," she said, closing her eyes.

She was so tired, and crammed on the hospital bed with Cole holding her in his warm, loving embrace, she slept more deeply than she had in months.

CHAPTER TWENTY-SEVEN
Cole

ONCE ISIS WAS HOME, the following days were a whirlwind of activity and diapers and crying and Marine Corps dependents paperwork. Isis and the baby lived with her parents, which meant they did most of the nighttime work, but Cortes had found a car for Cole right away, and he couldn't get behind the wheel quick enough.

The Jennings had given him a house key, so he was able to get to Isis's house early in the morning before Reveille and sunrise, do a feeding and diapering so Isis could sleep in, and spend some time with Aurore before he started his day.

After a week of running around, he spent a much calmer weekend with Isis and the baby. Sonia and Chaz were there, and between the three of them, all Isis had to do was sit on the couch and feed Aurore.

It was domestic bliss for Cole.

He had unpacked and figured out how to assemble the new stroller in the living room while Sonia and Chaz watched. Though Chaz had stopped glaring at him daily, his present gaze was more of a critical stare as Cole tried to figure out the complicated contraption. It had been a lot easier when the store display had been already put together at the store.

Isis couldn't stop laughing.

"Do you need help?" she teased.

He leveled his eyes at her. "I can take apart an M16 and put it back together with my eyes closed. I know I can do this."

Once he did have the stroller with the snap-in baby seat assembled and upright in the living room, both Isis and Sonia applauded. Cole's cheeks burned red in a mix of embarrassment and pride.

When Sonia asked about lunch, Cole offered to grab sandwiches at the local sub shop for everyone, and even Chaz asked for a turkey and ham on wheat and thanked him.

A trip to buy lunch wasn't his only reason for offering to go, however. He had made a firm decision the night he had cuddled Isis in the hospital.

Cole stopped at a nearby grocery store and grabbed a box of chocolates, a bouquet of flowers, and a package of strawberries. The checkout lady smiled knowingly at his purchases that screamed *I love you*.

With all the focus on the baby, he hadn't been able to show Isis that he was still in love with her and wanted to marry her. He didn't have a ring – hell he didn't know her ring size – but he could give her the romantic gifts and ask her again.

He would ask her every day if necessary.

And it was a good thing that Cortes managed to find him a good deal on a cheap car so he had enough to buy a small ring once he found a free moment.

The PX has a small jewelry section, he thought as he picked up their sandwiches and headed back to the house. *Maybe I can find something there. We can get it resized . . .*

Sonia and Chaz took their sandwiches outside, but Isis preferred to stay on the overstuffed couch. Cole dragged the coffee table close, so she had a place for her sandwich and sparkling lemon water drink. The baby dozed lightly in a small bassinet next to her.

After he had her food set up on the table, he excused himself to go back to his car and returned with her flowers and treats.

Isis's jaw dropped when he brought her all the gifts.

"What's all this?"

Cole dropped to his knee next to the table and held out the flowers. "I don't have a ring. So I brought you flowers because I had to have something. I know I've told you this before, but I want you to know now more than ever, I love you and can't imagine my life without you in it. Will you marry me?"

Her mouth was a breathless O as she stared at him, her celadon eyes searching his face.

"Cole . . . " she murmured.

"I know it's quick, and we've had a lot of changes, but nothing would make me happier than to come home to you and Aurore every day. Life is short, and I'm not going to squander it or what I have found with you. We're a family and we should be together."

"Oh, Cole," she breathed out as she leaned forward to press her forehead to his.

Several seconds passed before she finished her answer.

"Are you sure? What if we can't make this work?"

"Improvise. Overcome. Adapt. I think we've done that exceptionally well. And I want to continue to do that with you for the rest of my life."

She opened her mouth to speak, but he kissed her before any words came out, his full lips capturing hers in a tender kiss.

"I love you, Isis," he said in a breathless rush.

"I love you too, Cole. I can't believe it happened, but you have completely stolen my heart."

He closed his eyes, an odd sense of relief filling his soul, before recalled one problematic piece of information. He sat back on his heels.

"But you need to know something first. I have to deploy this summer, and I'll be gone again for six to eight months. I'm working on promoting to sergeant and hopefully a Stateside duty, but my squad needs me to fulfill my duties. Can you be married to a man who has to deploy? A man you can only spend a few months with at a time?"

At first, she looked shocked – probably at hearing he was being deployed again. She kept her face close to his while the lines around her eyes softened.

"When are you deploying?" she asked.

"In less than four months. That's the rumor. I should have confirmation by the end of May. I'm asking you to marry me because it will help you with the baby while I'm deployed, but also because I want to. I've never wanted anything more in my life, and I know that any deployment is manageable if I know I'm coming back to you. And her. But if you don't want to marry me, then I understand . . ."

A frosty clenching closed in on his chest. Was the deployment a deal breaker? Was that something she couldn't deal with? There had been not commitments with his other deployment – would being in a relationship complicate that?

He stopped breathing completely until she spoke again as she cupped his cheek with her cool palm.

"I think we did okay this time around. It all depends on what we do in those few months we have together, and if we work to make the most of it."

Cole straightened up on his knees. "Is that a yes?"

Isis grinned and nodded, her wispy hair falling out of her loose bun and into her eyes.

"Yes. Of course, it's a yes!"

His brow crinkled. "A yes? Are you sure?"

"At first I *wasn't* sure, or was worried I wasn't thinking straight because of hormones," she answered with a slight shrug. "Then I thought I had shown you how I felt. That it would be a yes if you asked."

Cole straightened and his blue gaze looked at her straight on. "I'm a Marine, Isis. I need direct commands."

"Okay then. Marine. Let's get married."

Chapter Twenty-Eight
Isis

Tick tock...

The clock in her head restarted, but this time for a different reason.

If they were going to get married, they should do it before Cole deployed, but Isis needed some time to get her body, her energy, her mind, her whole self, back.

But with the way this man had made her feel, renewed her heart after so many bad relationships, and did it all while she was pregnant while expecting nothing in return, she was going to figure out a way to get herself back on track and arrange a wedding.

Her ever-hopeful mother probably already had a venue and D.J. picked out.

"Really, did I hear you right? I need confirmation." Cole's eyes were like blue saucers that took over most of his face in disbelief.

His hands grasped the flowers, threatening to break their poor stems. She took the flowers from him and giggled under her breath as she set them next to her food.

"Yes. I said let's get married!"

Cole's face broke like the sun breaking the horizon on a brilliant summer morning. He wrapped his arms around her and kissed her.

"That was so much easier than this guessing game I've been playing. How soon?"

"How soon what?"

"I can get you a ring today and we can get married tomorrow. That's what I want, even though it might not be impossible. But I want you as my wife as soon as possible and before I deploy."

Her stomach fluttered at his brash declaration. "Maybe not tomorrow. Can we wait till I lose a little bit of a baby weight and can stand upright for any period of time? I'd rather not pass out walking down the aisle."

Cole exhaled a shaky breath. "Yeah, of course, whatever you need."

Leaning close to him again, Isis smiled and gazed into his wide eyes. For a moment, she wondered how he got the nickname Iron Maxton when he seemed to wear his emotions on his sleeve with her. There was nothing iron about him when it came to her.

"Give me a couple of weeks at least," she told him, "to get a dress and some flowers. And there's a park right next to the library with a beautiful pergola. Between my friends and my mother and me, we can get this together."

His long arms dropped and slid around her waist, holding her as if she was a delicate as glass.

"As long as it's you up there with me in front of an official, then nothing else matters."

Then he kissed her, a meeting of lips full of love and promise.

Isis

They were actually married two months later, on a Sunday, under that pergola. Isis looked like a fairy in her white, bohemian-styled dress she found at a beachside boutique.

Her mother was seated in the first row of white chairs with baby Aurore, who was wrapped in a pale green blanket, sleeping contentedly in her arm. Carly and Deidre beamed in simple champagne-hued dresses as her father, in a much happier mood, gleefully walked her toward the pergola.

The man's relief was as thick as cream.

Warm summer beach breezes washed over them as Cole waited under the pergola, a line of Marines next to him, all decked out in their formal dress blues. Was there anything as stunning as Marines in their dress uniform? As Isis shakily walked up to the pergola with her father, she didn't think so.

Cole was the image of the perfect gentleman, his curly hair covered by his white hat and his long, toned body and wide shoulders accentuated by the formal navy-blue coat. Pure joy suffused his face as her father gave Isis's hand to Cole.

He gripped it as if he would never let her go. And she never wanted him to.

"Are you ready?" he asked in a low voice as she moved next to him on the wooden platform.

Her joyful face matched his. "For something that didn't go according to plan, this is everything I could have asked for. I am more than ready, Cole."

Isis and Cole

That night, they checked into the same seedy motel near the *Easy Company* bar. Her mother was outright horrified at their choice, and Carly and Deidre thought she was crazy for choosing that as her honeymoon hotel. Deidre had even offered to use her credit card points to get her a nice hotel right on the beach.

"One with room service," Deidre had commented dryly.

Isis only grinned at her.

She didn't need some five star hotel with room service.

She and Cole wanted to go back to where they had started. They had slept together twice since she had been cleared by the doctor, but those were quick and furtive encounters when they had the house to themselves and the baby was thankfully asleep. Nothing like having an entire room to themselves with no one else around to disturb them like they did at the motel.

A week earlier, she had mentioned she was worried about going back to that room. Cole's thick brown eyebrows crinkled across his forehead as his head tilted slightly.

"I know the décor was atrocious and the bed sagged, but why are you worried about it?"

Isis shrugged one shoulder. "That night, it was like a dream, Cole. What if it's not as good when we go back? I kinda don't want to shatter that dream."

He had moved closer to her, embracing her in a bear-like hug that made it surprisingly easy to sink into his otherwise hardened body.

"That dream kept me alive in the desert. It was something to look forward to when I came home. That night gave me hope, and if nothing else ever rises to meet that, it's okay with me, because we still have that night." He had kissed the top of her forehead then pressed his finger under her chin so her face rose to meet his. The edge of his lips curled. "But I'm going to keep trying as hard as I can to have each night with you rise to that. Try hard and *a lot*."

Isis had slyly smirked at his suggestive joke, and he had kissed her, his full lips sucking and slanting, his tongue reaching out to caress hers.

Much like he was kissing her now at the motel door, his lips owning her tongue, her mouth, her jaw as he fumbled with the key card at the door. Isis let her head fall back so his lips could move farther down her neck to her tanned chest, to the light swell of her breasts under her dress corset.

His aura surrounded her, smelling of sunlight and cologne and Cole's musky, intoxicating scent tinged with beach air. She cupped the back of his head to bring him closer.

He groaned deep in his chest, his mouth licking and nipping and biting, and the door clicked. They practically spilled into the ivory and avocado green room.

They parted for a brief moment to stare at the room, at the motel where this had all started, and when her eyes circled back to Cole, he was staring at her with fiery blue intensity.

Then she was in his arms as he lifted her easily onto the bed. With one hand, he undid the buttons on his formal coat and he tugged her dress skirt up with the other. She wore creamy thigh highs, and his entire body froze when he discovered them.

His long-fingered hand caressed the inside of her thigh, trailing heated lines of desire up her legs to the lacy edge of the thigh-highs.

"No matter what else happens tonight, you are keeping these on," he said in a thick, gruff tone.

His fingers continued their sensuous dance up her thigh to the edge of her cream-colored panties. With a brief pause to remove his dress blues coat and toss it on the nearby chair with his hat, he returned his finger to the tender apex of her legs.

The lacy edge of her gown draped around her hips, exposing her entire lower body to his feasting eyes. The icy blue drew her in, and her insides fluttered. She lifted up on her elbow and with one hand, cupped his pulsing erection over his pants. He was hot and thick and more than ready.

"I want to draw this out, make this last," he said in a strained voice. "But I want you so bad, Isis. I need you more than I need the air I breath, that I don't think I can."

She squeezed his throbbing hard-on slightly, and he bowed his head and groaned.

"We have all night, babe. We can go as fast or slow as you desire."

Her words dripped with heady passion, and her voice urged him on. With one hand he unfastened his belt and zipper while he yanked down her delicate wedding panties with the other.

It was like an animal roared up from him – the heat of his hands and body, his deep groaning, and the urgent need that wafted off him like a humming electrical current – and that animalistic desire made her dizzy and her sex wet.

Everything about him made her excited, something she had to control in their daily lives through sheer force of will. Sometimes just glancing in his direction made her insides flutter.

But now, here in this room where it all started, she could be as wild and lusty as she wanted. She didn't have to hide, she didn't have to wonder – Cole was here, married to her, and he was hers in body and soul as much as she was his.

As he shifted to remove his pants, she leaned up and unbuttoned his dress shirt. She longed to see him, see all of him. Even if he couldn't wait long enough to get her gown off.

Her hands slid over the powerful planes of his chest. His patch of curly brown chest hair tickled her fingers. Cole groaned again.

"Lie back. I told you the day I returned that I came back for you. It was always you, Isis." Cole's voice was breathless.

She leaned back and shifted so her hips could meet his, and her hand tickled down his flat abs to his dick, hot and bulging against her fingers. She gripped his thick arousal, feeling the glistening tip, and slid her hand up and down until he bowed his forehead against hers and shuddered.

"Always you, Isis," he whispered, his breath warm on her cheek, then he lifted her hips and pressed forward to shove his engorged erection into her, sliding deep until he filled her completely.

Isis threw her head back and arched at the heady sensation of fullness, of body meeting body, of being joined as one. Her fingers clung to his hands as if she might pull him in deeper.

That was all it took to release the animal he'd been trying to contain. His hips worked, thrusting between her thighs again and again, in a hard cadence of pressure and pulling and a steady mumbling of her name. With each thrust, his groin rubbed against her pink pearl, dragging over and over until the pleasurable vibrations that started at her core spread to her fingers, her toes, her face, bursting through her in quaking wave.

His hand moved, caressing her breast, brushing over the peaked nipple that had popped free of her dress. He curved over her and trailed his fingers upward until his hand cupped her face.

"Always you," Cole was chanting as he moved above her, like a mantra as he worshipped her body and wracked her core. This was more than sex, more than the joining of two bodies, but rather a raw and dire hunger for each other. A desperate need that had to be fulfilled.

She peeked through her closed eyes at his body, each defined muscle of his arms and chest shifting with each move. His narrowed eyes, however, remained fixed on her, as if he couldn't tear his tender blue gaze from her, as if he was memorizing every feature, the feel of her body, the intensity of her touch.

Cole slid his other hand down her leg and grabbed under her knee, bending it. He trapped her bent leg under his arm so her hips shifted and spread wider for him, giving him more access to her wet opening and thrusting impossibly deeper. As his thick cock slid out, it dragged over the tender parts of her sheath, caressing her most sensitive spot and she arched her back as he withdrew.

Then he slammed back in, surging over the spot, then again and again.

"Always you, Isis," he still chanted in a voice that sounded far away.

Everything inside her body burst into flame as she dug her nails into him, the bedding, anything she could grab as she gasped and moaned and called out his name.

His breathing and the tempo of his movements changed as she clung to him, careening through ecstasy. Cole's movements became frenzied as he thrust and thrust, gritting his teeth as his cock flexed inside her and his own exquisite orgasm erupted inside her. He stiffened, every perfect muscle in his body hovering as he poured himself into her.

Then they were still, weightless as they rode out the moment of rapture that consumed them.

With a shuddering groan, Cole moved his long, naked body next to her, brushing lengths of her rumpled dress to the side as he curled into her. He cupped her exposed breast, and his breath was hot on her damp neck. The moment was ideal, matching their first night together, or so she thought. Then he spoke and made it perfection.

"Always you, Isis."

The End

Love this sweet and steamy romance? Then read book 2 — Her Irresistible Guardian

An Excerpt from Undercover

"Where's Hawk? Get 'im here." Jerod's voice was like a gunshot to the men in the nearly empty house, and they jumped when Jerod spoke.

Jerod expected it. As the boss of the Red Hill gang this side of the freeway, he was used to having his guys jump when he spoke.

His guy Hawk, though, wasn't at the house where Jerod maintained his operations, and that pissed him off. He liked Hawk. He *needed* Hawk. No one else had eyes like this guy who managed to see everything and remember everyone. That's how he got his nickname – he had eyes like a bird of prey. And that was the kind of guy Jerod needed to keep his low-level dealers under control and on track. Who knew what those fuckers would do if left to their own devices?

Jerod had seen too much in his time with the gang to let a stupid dealer fuck it up. So Jerod recruited Hawk to do that grunt work so Jerod could focus on more important things. Hawk saw everything and was huge enough to keep his street dealer safe and accountable.

Like how to get more Butterfly out on the streets.

It had been good business so far. Butterfly mixed with the perfect amount of fentanyl. Enough to get a user hooked with one hit, but not enough to kill them. They called it Butterfly for the image used on the package and the changing nature of the drug and the single hit to get hooked. That's why he stayed away from heroin and a few other fentanyl laced drugs. A dead customer wasn't a paying customer, and all Jerod's customers paid.

Hawk was the reason for that. Those hard eyes on a big man. . . no one messed with Hawk.

Which meant no one messed with Jerod.

It was a sweet deal.

But he needed Hawk here to check in with a street dealer who was late on his payment, and his enforcer was nowhere to be found. Jerod could deal with the dealer, but he had larger tasks on hand. This was Hawk's job.

Jerod ran his stout fingers through his dark brown hair. Where was he?

As if by magic, Hawk sauntered into Jerod's dingy upstairs office.

He didn't even knock, like most of Jerod's cowering crew did. Nope, not this huge fucker. He strode in with his brown hair brushed back like he'd just preened in the mirror, his plain blue t-shirt tight across his chest, and those eyes, a green-brown gaze that missed nothing. Jerod couldn't help but smile at that thought.

"Yeah, boss?" Hawk asked, his deep baritone rolling across the room.

Jerod smiled wider. Who the fuck wouldn't do whatever this guy said? Hawk had been a rare find for Jerod, and since he'd come on a few months ago after being down on his luck, business had run smoothly.

Just like Jerod wanted.

"Stickle hasn't checked in. He owes me three bones. He should be working the Browning Avenue corner. Bring either the money or his head. I don't care which."

He did care – he wanted the money. Dead dealers didn't pay, either.

Hawk nodded once and ducked back out the door.

Jerod sat back in his worn office chair, watching him leave.

Hawk had been quite a find, indeed.

Officer Liam Turner, street name Hawk, took the stairs two at a time before bursting out the front door with his task from Jerod.

Undercover work wasn't for the weak willed. The strength and sheer effort it took to keep up the facade 24-7 wore on a person, and hard. Unlike other officers on the Tustin Police Department or Orange County Sheriff coordination team, Officer Turner had an easier time of it. No wife, no kids, no family local, so he was able to blend in and not have any part of his mind preoccupied with obligations of the heart.

He was all business when he took off the uniform and put on his plain clothes t-shirt and jeans and blended into the gangland underbelly. What there was of it in Orange County.

It helped that he was tall and well-built. Well, those words were understatements. A hair over six foot six, and a body-builder physique — he weighed in at more than 250 pounds. Gangs liked to have enforcers on their crews, and needless to say, Liam fit that bill to perfection. His street name Hawk, though, he hadn't expected that. Compared to half-drugged, half-scared dealers and low-level crew, who had to keep their attention focused on what they were doing, lest they end up a beaten pulp in the gutter or worse, Hawk's attention was routinely focused on the dealers, the crew, and that up-line. It was needed for his undercover work, but the local boss found value in it, too.

In fact, the only thing distracting Liam right now was the gang task-force's recent information regarding who the higher-ups were and the take-down the task force was actively working on.

Not that the information or the take down team changed anything for Liam – he kept his eyes open, his ears sharp, and learned everything he could. They were so close, and if anything, that encouraged Liam to pay better attention to the members of the Red Hill Crew.

He turned the corner, heading south to Browning, and slipped his second Trac phone from a pocket he had sewn inside his jeans. He used his crew phone for Jerod's work, but when he needed to reach his contact, he needed a non-traceable phone that could be easily destroyed.

Diaz picked up on the second ring.

"Diaz," his task-force contact answered in a clipped voice. Everything about Mario Diaz was clipped. He didn't mess around.

"It's Turner. I'm going after a dealer who didn't show. Heads up if he doesn't have the cash."

That meant Hawk had to use more physical inducement to get the dealer to pony up the cash if he didn't have it.

"Gotcha. Keep it on the down low and don't do too much. Any more word on the big bosses for Red Hill? Who are they under?"

"Nothing since yesterday, but after I deal with this guy, I'll head back to Jerod's with my mouth shut and eyes and ears open."

"Copy that," Diaz confirmed. "Stay safe and check in tomorrow."

"Copy that," Liam agreed and snapped the phone shut. He tucked it into his secret pocket and stepped around another corner onto Browning Street.

Read Undercover today!

Excerpt from Charming

Excerpt from *Charming*

MARIAH SLAPPED HER PHONE before it emitted another trilling beep. She had lowered the volume as far as she dared to still be able to wake up for class, but in the dark of night, the ringer still sounded far too loud.

The snoring body next to her grunted and Mariah froze. The apartment was quiet — she even held her breath to make sure she didn't make as sound either. Once the body settled, Mariah lifted the covers and slipped out, as stealthy as a thief.

And wasn't that what she was doing? Thieving her time away from Derek? Mariah tiptoed to the narrow walk-in closet, and only when the door was secure did she turn on the light.

She blinked in the sudden illumination and released the breath she held as she pulled down the loose tank top, hunter green duster sweater, and dress slacks she had selected the night before. Mariah hated eight a.m. classes and laid out her outfit the night before to cut back on the time it took to get ready.

Once dressed, she shut off the light and slipped to the kitchen to make a small pot of tea, then closed herself in the bathroom to apply a quick layer of makeup.

For a college professor in her late 20s, makeup should have been an area of expertise for Mariah, but having spent much of her late teens and early adult hood with her nose in a book, makeup had remained a mystery to her.

She was fortunate, however, that her lightly tanned skin only needed a quick application of BB cream and makeup that came in iridescent plastic kits, so all she had to do was open one kit and everything else was ready — eyeliner, shadow, mascara, a hint of blush and lip gloss. Her dark brown eyes were easily smoky, so that saved time as well.

Then came the bane of her existence — a fluffy mound of ash-blonde hair that was half wavy, half curly, and always a frizzy mess. Mariah called it her triangle mess. She pulled it into a bun or a banana clip nearly every day and called it good. Her hair was a disaster. She decided on a clip to keep it under control. It was too early to deal with her hair-disaster.

Zipping up her books, she grabbed a to-go cup of tea and her purse waiting by the front door, then peeked in her purse.

Her keys weren't in her purse.

Where the hell are my keys?

She pressed her head against the apartment door and exhaled.

In the bedroom. She had retrieved a book from her car last night before bed and left the keys on her bedside table.

Fuck.

Mariah pulled off her boots and, leaving them by the front door, slipped back into the bedroom which was still dark thanks to the room darkening curtains. She palmed the keys so they wouldn't jingle and made it to the bedroom doorway.

But she missed her count and banged the side of her head against the door jamb.

She held her breath again, sure that the banging woke Derek, but he continued to snore. His late night was paying off in her favor. Rubbing the side of her head, she made it back to the front door, zipped her boots back on, and left.

Escaped was more like it.

Once she was in her car, she fully breathed again.

"I can't live like this," she told herself.

She was an adjunct professor, making enough money to support herself, a feminist who was supposed to be a role model for her young college students, yet she lived with a narcissistic emotional abuser who gaslighted her on a regular basis.

Mariah was not proud.

Glancing at the clock in her car, she took a sip of her cooling tea and pulled out to the street toward campus.

Mariah's mind drifted as she drove the short trip. Not for the first time, she asked herself what she was doing with Derek. The past few weeks had become a living hell with the man, and she was still letting him sleep over and dictate how to live in her own home.

What the hell is wrong with me?

Why was she letting him do this? She wasn't that type of person. She didn't see herself as that type of person.

In fact, she'd been called a bitch to her face more than once. And she reveled in the term. Why not own it?

What had happened over the past years that made her think she deserved someone like Derek? That was the lone conclusion she could draw — that subconsciously she believed she wasn't deserving of someone better.

Who the hell am I?

But what if her subconscious was telling her something? What if she was only worthy of someone like Derek?

They had met at a bar, of all places.

By God, shouldn't that have been a clue?

Nothing but a meat market, and two of her friends outside campus dragged Mariah there on a Karaoke night. A tallish blond with a decent physique, at least what she could discern from the button down he wore — took the stage and belted out a decent rendition of *Don't Stop Believing*. Mariah had loved it and ended up cheering louder than anyone else in the bar.

The three shots of Fireball hadn't hurt either.

She got his number, made out with him in the parking lot, and called him later in the week.

Most of their dates had been to bars. That should have been her first clue.

But he was so sexy — with light eyes that squinted in a come-hither way that reached into her chest and squeezed her heart.

When was the last time she'd felt that with him? Mariah couldn't recall.

And he had a great job, so he wasn't leeching off her.

Slowly he'd started making requests of her, about her apartment or how she lived. And as much as she hated herself for it, she'd begun to walk on eggshells around him.

And they didn't do anything together. They didn't watch movies and eat popcorn on the couch. They didn't go to any campus events, even though the music festivals were fun. They didn't have long conversations late into the night. They'd eaten out together all of two times. No dates to the park, nothing. Was she overly romantic, or misguided to think that relationships should be more? All they shared was the bar and the bed.

The bar and bed.

He'd been decent enough in bed to start. Giving it his all the first time or two.

Mariah tapped her fingers on her steering wheel as she waited at a light. She also couldn't recall the last time she came when he was pumping into her. Lately, she'd begun to push him away, using the old "I have a headache" line.

Yeah. Something needed to be done.

She was done.

Start the Campus Heat Series and Charming Today!

Marine Corps Report

I would like to extend a heartfelt thank you to all of you for taking a chance and reading this new series. That you, dear reader, took the chance to read this military romantic tale makes the risk worth it.

Recently, I have been teaching on a large Marine base, and my encounters with this amazing people of our military inspired me to write this series. Add to that, my hubby is a former Marine, and this series seemed to make sense. This series is dedicated to all those who serve in uniform! Many of the characters and scenarios are based off what I have seen in the course of being on base and from stories my hubby has shared. I hope you enjoy them!

I would also like to thank my kids and family in general for always supporting me. They always assumed writing was my real job. To my encouraging children, Mommy has always been an author. And my mom, who saw her daughter get a degree in English, of all things, and made no judgements, and instead remained confident that her daughter would be successful even with such an inauspicious field of study.

Finally, I would like to thank Michael, the man in my life who has been so supportive of my career shift to focus more on writing, and who makes a great sounding board for ideas. He is also my hero, and I listen for that sound of his safe return home every night.

If you liked this book, please leave a review! Reviews can be bread and butter for an author, and I appreciate your comments and feedback!

About the Author

M.D. Dalrymple, aka Michelle Deerwester-Dalrymple, is a professor of writing and an author. She started reading when she was 3 years old, writing when she was 4, and published her first poem at age 16. She has written articles and essays on a variety of topics, including several texts on writing for middle and high school students. She has written over seventy books under a variety of pen names and is also slowly working on a novel inspired by actual events. Her Glen Highland romance series books have won *The Top Ten Academy Awards* for books, *Top 50 Indie Books for 2019*, and the *2021 N.N. Light Book Awards*. She lives in California with her family of seven.

Find Michelle on your favorite social media sites and sign up for her newsletter at this website: https://linktr.ee/mddalrympleauthor

The Highlander's Legacy

The Highlander's Return

Her Knight's Second Chance

The Highlander's Vow

Her Knight's Christmas Gift

Her Outlaw Highlander

Outlaw Highlander Found

Outlaw Highlander Home

<u>As M.D. Dalrymple - Men in Uniform</u>

Night Shift – Book 1

Day Shift – Book 2

Overtime – Book 3

Holiday Pay – Book 4

School Resource Officer – book 5

Undercover – book 6

Holdover – book 7

<u>Campus Heat</u>

Charming – Book 1

Tempting – Book 2

Infatuated -- Book 3

Craving – Book 4

Alluring – Book 5

<u>*Men In Uniform: Marines*</u>

Her Desirable Defender – Book 1

Printed in Great Britain
by Amazon